MW00987923

ROAD TRIPPIN'

A LESBIAN ROMANCE NOVEL

NICOLETTE DANE

ROAD TRIPPIN'

Having just finalized her divorce, Dana Darling feels uncertain and lost in life. As a woman in her mid-30s, where does she go from here? But Dana knows the divorce was the right move and these feelings inside of her can no longer be ignored.

When her good friend Maggie invites her on a road trip out west, Dana's eyes really start to open. Maggie is a firecracker, a sweet, pretty, and sensual woman who Dana deeply admires. And while Maggie has always been open and free, Dana has never been able to come out to her friend and admit her true feelings.

Out on the open road with a fun and flirty woman like Maggie, Dana truly begins to see the path ahead of her. Will the freedom she feels on this road trip allow her to finally open up and be free herself?

CONTENTS

Copyright © 2016 Nicolette Dane

This book is a work of fiction. Names, characters, places, and incidents either are products of the author's imagination or are used fictitiously. Any resemblance to actual persons, living or dead, events, or locales is entirely coincidental. All rights reserved.

Previously published as Restless on a Road Trip.

ABOUT THE AUTHOR

Nicolette Dane landed in Chicago after studying writing in New York City. Flitting in and out of various jobs without finding her place, Nico decided to choose herself and commit to writing full-time. Her stories are contemporary scenarios of blossoming lesbian romance and voyeuristic tales meant to give you a peep show into the lives of sensual and complicated women. If you're a fan of uplifting and steamy lesbian passion, you've found your new favorite author.

www.nicolettedane.com

SIGN UP FOR NICO'S MAILING LIST!

If you'd like to be notified of all new releases from Nicolette Dane and receive FREE books, head over to Nico's website and sign up for her mailing list right now!

www.nicolettedane.com

ONE

*W*hat a year. I think it was about a year ago this month, July, that I had told my husband I wanted a divorce. I say that with a bit of ease but it was a very difficult decision to come to and even more difficult to actually speak out loud. Paul was flabbergasted. To him it must have come from nowhere. But to me it was something that had been brewing for a long time. Probably before I had even met Paul.

There's a time in your life where it seems everybody you know is getting married. It happens quickly over the course of a couple of years and if you're not careful you might get swept up in that madness. I think that's what happened to me. I mean, I take responsibility for it all but I sort of fell in line when I really shouldn't have. It was Paul who got the marriage bug, as we had just gone through wedding season — he had been in his buddy's wedding — and I think he was just ready to shuck the uncertainty of what our future would hold.

He proposed to me and for some unknown reason I said yes.

But I didn't feel it in my heart. I guess I just felt a weird obligation. We had been dating for 4 years, living together for 2 of those years, and Paul was kind of an old school type of guy who was interested in building a big family. I never thought about having kids. I saw some of my girlfriends go through it, the toll it took on their bodies, the stress and the difficulty, and I just felt, "you know, that's not for me."

And look, between us, the sex was never good. I don't blame Paul for that, I blame myself. It was always odd for me, it never quite felt right. And I could say that same thing for all the guys I'd been with, which was a low number of 3, including Paul. It just didn't seem to give me the kind of fun and enjoyment I had been told it should. It was really confusing. I mean, *really*. Friends would talk about sex, gush about how much they loved it with their guys. "Oh, I love that moment when he pushes into me." It just made me queasy. It made me panic.

I felt broken. I felt like a failure. And after I was married, I felt like a fraud. I could really only stand a year of it before it started giving me anxiety, more intense anxiety than I'd ever felt, and I knew then that I had to get out. Paul was trying to convince me to have a baby and meanwhile I just felt supremely trapped. I couldn't explain it to myself. Every time I tried to analyze it, it just worried me and stressed me out and made me feel like an idiot.

But the one thing I was sure of, the one thing I knew to be true, was that this marriage was not for me.

Partner to that time in your life where all your friends are getting married is that time when they begin getting divorces. What's the statistic? Around 50% of marriages end in divorce? I think that number is so high because of people like me who get married not because they really want to, but because they feel they're supposed to. That's definitely a recipe for unrest and subsequently divorce. I take the blame, though. I accept it. This was totally on me.

Paul was obviously upset when I told him I wanted to split. He wanted to reconcile, to figure it out, but I knew deep down, *in my soul*, some sort of intrinsic motivation submersed within me, that this was not right. And I told him that. I told him I had made a mistake, that it was *me*, that I was sorry and I knew I had ruined things. He was as understanding as someone put through that would be. Since we'd only been married a year and we didn't have any joint property or any money, we decided for a clean break. A couple of friends hinted at me trying to get alimony, as Paul had the better job, but that made me feel even grosser than I already felt. I just wanted out.

It was all so hard. I never want to go through that again. But at the same time, once the divorce was finalized — so, just a few weeks ago — I felt this crazy weight lifted off me. No longer did I feel claustrophobic. I felt free and unencumbered. I felt like I could breathe again, like I could be me. And even though I was now 35 and single and not sure what was going to happen next in my life, I was certain that I was beginning to walk down the right path to discover who I was and who I really wanted to be.

When I told her that the divorce had been finalized, my very good friend Maggie invited me out to a hip restaurant in her neighborhood to celebrate. Maggie lived on the northside of Chicago, in Andersonville, while I had been living in Logan Square and crashing with another friend while I got my life figured out. Ever since I began dating Paul, Maggie and I didn't really see each other as often as we had in the past. That seems to happen when you shack up and start orchestrating a life with someone else. Your friends seem to fade away.

But Maggie always brought a smile to my face. She was firecracker. A pretty little blonde chick with fun energy. I say little because Maggie was 5'1" and barely cracked 100 pounds. She was hip and cool, a professor at Columbia College teaching fashion design and drawing. We had met in college and roomed together our sophomore year. Maggie was one of my oldest friends and I loved her dearly. Every time I thought of her, it brought a smile to my face.

Sitting across from me in the booth, a light fashioned into a mason jar hanging down between us to provide a bit of illumination in the darkened restaurant, Maggie pushed her black browline glasses up her nose and took a sip of her wine glass. She grinned over at me with a happiness bubbling within her. Even though she knew I was sad, she also knew that her energy could help coax some happiness back into me.

"So that's how it went down," I admitted, fingering my

own wine glass between my two hands, resting on the table. "It's done."

"Dana," said Maggie, like she was leveling with me. "I think this was the right decision."

"I know," I admitted. "I feel so much better. But I also feel so freaking guilty."

"Look," she said. "I was at your wedding. I knew then that something wasn't right. But, c'mon, who stands up at a wedding and protests it?" Maggie chuckled to herself. "I'm not *that* person."

"Well, maybe you could have said something *before* the wedding."

"That's crazy," said Maggie. "How does anybody *really* know what's going on inside anyone else's head? You just gotta let people be themselves." She took another long sip from her glass and her beautiful blonde ringlets bounced effortlessly. I always admired her hair. She was a natural blonde, through I think her stylist gave her a bit of help with some lowlights, and she had such a pretty face. I admit, I thought about how attractive Maggie was a lot.

"It's all over now," I sighed. "I know I seem sad, but I really am happy about it. I'm happy that I'm out of that thing. It just didn't feel right for me. But I am sad because I kind of feel like I ruined Paul's life."

"You didn't," said Maggie with empathy. "I'm sure it's hard but he'll move on."

"Yeah," I sighed.

"So what are you going to do now?" she asked. Maggie

reached out and picked a kalamata olive from the small plate between us.

"I really have no idea," I said.

"Work okay?"

"Work's okay," I said. "It's summer, so we're a little slow but it's fine."

"I'm free for the summer," said Maggie with a grin. "I love teaching at a college. I mean, sure, I could teach summer classes for more money but I much prefer to have the time off to do whatever I want."

"And what are you doing with this free time?" I asked, letting a smile wash over me. I was tired of talking about myself. I wanted to talk about Maggie.

"Didn't I tell you?" she said with heightened enthusiasm. "I'm doing a road trip out to Boulder to see my friend Piper."

"I love that name," I said. "Piper. Wasn't she *more* than a friend at one point?"

"Yeah," said Maggie, lightly blushing and trying to stifle a laugh. "She was my girlfriend first, *that* didn't work out, so now we're just friends. It's much better this way."

"So you're driving out to Colorado alone to see Piper?" I surmised. "That sounds fun. How long?"

"About three weeks," she said. "I may continue on out west because I haven't really seen that part of the country. Maybe Salt Lake City," Maggie mused. "Have you ever been there?"

"No," I said.

"I hear there's a lot of good hiking out there," she said.

"There's this hot spring I read about that I'd *really* love to visit."

"I can't believe you're doing this all alone," I said. "Is Piper tagging along?"

"Sadly, no," said Maggie. "She's only taking a few days off work. So I'll only get to spend a little time with her."

"That sounds like a lot of fun," I said. "That's going to be an excellent trip."

After a pause, Maggie's eyes lit up, brow raised, a smile growing on her face. I looked over at her and knew exactly what she was thinking.

"No," I said, holding up a finger before she could speak. "There's no way I could do that right now."

"You *have* to," said Maggie. "Dana, this is the perfect time for you to do something like this."

"I don't even know if I can get the time of work," I lamented. "I don't have much money."

"You said it's slow right now," countered Maggie. "Do you have the PTO?"

"I do," I said slowly. "Maybe not 3 *weeks* worth."

"Didn't you tell me a few years back that your boss went through a messy divorce?" asked Maggie cagily.

"I did," I said. I could follow Maggie's every thought. We'd known each other so long and been so close that she was easy for me to read.

"*Well,*" she said. "Maybe you could, you know, test the waters with her and maybe negotiate yourself a little time off to deal with your own divorce."

"You are just incorrigible," I said. This really gave

Maggie a tickle. Her smile was infectious. Her full pink lips peeling back and exposing her teeth.

"I don't even think we're having a discussion about this anymore," said Maggie. "This is serendipity. The stars are aligned perfectly for you, my dear, and this is going to be the summer of Dana. You need to have some fun."

"It really does sound like fun," I admitted cautiously.

"I love it!" beamed Maggie, swiftly reaching across the table and grabbing my hand. She squeezed lovingly. "Dana, we're doing this. I'm leaving in 10 days and you're coming with me."

"I don't know…" I hummed. Deep down, I really wanted to do this. I would love to spend some extended time with Maggie. We hadn't been as close in the recent past than we were throughout our history and it would be a great opportunity to reconnect. And as I considered this possibility, I suddenly felt something really strange come over me. It was a fire within me, some kind of weird desire to be with Maggie. Like, I wanted to spend every waking hour with her. It was a feeling I'd definitely felt before, it was memorable, but it was also something suppressed and hidden.

"It's decided," said Maggie, waving me off. "We're doing this," she repeated, even firmer this time.

"Okay," I said, coming around, letting my smile show. "All right, Maggie. We're doing this."

"Hell yeah!" said Maggie, maybe a little too loud for the quiet restaurant we were in. She looked around suddenly and laughed at herself. "You're not going to regret this. Road trips are the *best*."

"Yeah," I said, really beginning to feel happy about it. It was a palpable happiness and welcomed. Maggie was right. This was something I needed. The stars had aligned and I was going to just let it happen. I smiled across the table at her adoringly and Maggie smiled back. That fair visage of hers, her pretty little features, they soothed me.

BEFORE I KNEW IT, Maggie and I were packing up her SUV with our things. It was early, 6AM, and I had that amazing feeling of adventure that you always get on the morning of a road trip. You feel absolutely free. You feel like you have no responsibilities. You feel like you're open to anything and everything. It's almost as though you're not the person you usually were. You were a way more open-minded person, someone who was just ready to accept whatever the world happened to throw at you.

Maggie had the driver's side door open and she was reaching inside, just her backside and legs sticking out. She was dressed in short black running shorts, her legs slim and bare, all the way down to some small red canvas slip-ons. Once she popped back out of the car, wearing a half-zip long sleeve athletic top, she grinned over at me and held up a small dangly cord.

"This connects my phone to the stereo," she said. Her blonde hair was tied up in a thick pony, those geek chic glasses over her eyes. "I lost it between the seats the other day."

NICOLETTE DANE

I couldn't stop myself from thinking about her butt, covered by the thin material of her shorts. The image of her reaching deep into the car was etched into my mind. But I got a hold of myself and pushed the thoughts down.

"Is that it?" I said. "Are we ready to go?"

"Get excited!" said Maggie. "We're hittin' the road!"

Maggie had a nice, spacious SUV with a black leather interior. The car was a handful of years old, but it still looked new and fancy. It was the perfect road tripping machine. The cargo cab in the back had plenty of room for our bags. The comfort and ease of it all brought a smile to my face. We were really doing this. We were driving out west.

It had been a long time since my last road trip, and I wouldn't even call that a proper road trip like Maggie and I were embarking on. The last time I'd been in a car for an extended period was when Paul and I drove from Chicago to northern Michigan to spend a week with some friends at a lakehouse. That was about an 8 hour trip. This trip, however, side by side with Maggie, was going to take a couple of days between stops. This was the kind of trip that you do in your own time. If you want to stop, you stop. If you feel like pressing on, well, that's just what you do. It was the open road and I was open to the experience.

"Will you reach into my purse and get my sunglasses?" asked Maggie, looking over at me quickly before returning her eyes to the road. "They're in a hardshell case."

"On it," I said. I reached back and dug into her bag, as instructed, pulled out the case and removed her sunglasses from it. Maggie smiled at me as we made the exchange and she slipped the big plastic frames over her eyes.

"That's better," she said. "The sun is already pretty bright today."

"Maggie, I've got to admit this to you," I said. "I'm really happy you convinced me to do this. I'm feeling super excited about it."

"That's right, girl," she grinned. "Don't you just feel like a total load has been lifted off you?"

"Totally," I affirmed. As we pulled onto the highway, albeit slow from the morning Chicago traffic, I felt like this trip was now becoming real. No turning back.

"So we're going to power through today," said Maggie. "Southern Illinois and Iowa are going to be *boring*. Farmlands. That's what I've heard, anyway," she said.

"That's all right," I said with a smile. "We can just catch up."

"Right," she said. "We should get into Omaha and hook up with our AirBnB host around dinner time."

"You reserved an AirBnB?" I asked.

"I told you, Dana," she said. "I got this."

"You got this."

"I'm gonna show you a fabulous time on this trip and take your mind off all that crap you've had going on," said Maggie. "Just chill out and have fun."

"I think I can handle that," I said. It did feel nice to relinquish control and let Maggie handle the particulars. There had been so much on my mind lately that I could use the free headspace.

"Damn traffic," muttered Maggie absently as she looked over her shoulder and then merged. "Do you know one of the coolest things about going to Colorado to hang out?" she asked.

"What's that?"

"Legal weed!" Maggie said and then broke into a laugh.

"Weed?" I said, laughing along with her. "You're crazy, Mags. I haven't done that in, like, 6 or 7 years."

"But it's legal now," she said. "I mean, we totally have to go to the store and buy it. Just for the experience."

"The experience," I reiterated. "Sure."

"They have crazy stuff out there," she said. "Piper's told me so much. Not just, you know, the plant material. But gummy candy, and tinctures, and even topical ointments and patches."

"Patches?"

"Yeah," Maggie said. "Piper had her wisdom teeth out recently and instead of popping the pills her doctor prescribed, she got these patches that she stuck to her arm and they helped mitigate the pain."

"That's some futuristic stuff," I said. "Sounds like Colorado is really taking this weed science thing seriously."

"I know, *right?*" Maggie laughed again. "It's so *interesting* to me. I've got to see what it's like."

"Okay," I relented. "I'll go to one of those stores with you, but I don't want to get obliterated or anything. I'm sure the weed out there is really strong."

"We'll be good." Maggie looked over to me and grinned.

Despite the sunglasses covering her face, I knew she had the devil in her eyes.

"Sure," I mused, shaking my head. I felt a great sense of excitement brewing inside of me at our little back and forth. And when I looked at Maggie in the driver seat, her small frame sitting there deep in the black leather, hands atop the wheel, guiding us through the beginning of our trip, I couldn't help but look down to her bare thighs. Maggie's shorts had ridden up on her and exposed even more of her smooth legs and I kept peering over at them out of the corner of my eye. She was so small and beautiful.

There was just something about this woman. I couldn't quite tell you what it was. But she made me feel different. I was drawn to her, you know? Like, in some sort of physical way. I always caught myself admiring her, thinking about her, wondering what it might be like to touch her. If I could have reached over and stroked her bare leg, I definitely would have. It's what I wanted. And then I could just slide my hand up the thin fabric of those shorts…

"Do you feel like you're moving on from Paul?" asked Maggie suddenly, though with a hint of trepidation. Her words broke my reverie and I felt somewhat caught off guard.

"I, um…" I said, stammering. "I don't know," I surmised after a moment. "I mean, as I think about it I'm not sure I was ever really, you know, *gung ho* about him."

"That's so crazy to hear you say," she admitted. "Because, Dana, I *felt* that."

"Yeah?"

"Yeah!" she said. "There was always something off there."

"Right," I said.

"So what *are* you looking for in a guy?" Maggie said with enthusiasm. I could tell she was eager to bond like we had in the past. This trip for her had originated as a respite from her normal life but had become something else entirely with me joining in.

"I don't know, Maggie," I said, feeling put on the spot. "I don't know anything about guys. I don't know if I want to talk about this."

"Fine, fine," she said, lifting one hand off the wheel and holding it up. "Don't hold back on this trip, though," Maggie continued. "I'm ready to deal with whatever you want to deal with. We're going to create some memories," she said, once again looking over to me with a wide grin. "And I think both of our lives are going to be irrevocably changed from this."

"I think you're right."

IT WAS a long drive through Iowa but I'd be lying if I said I didn't find the green farmland beautiful. Yeah, it can be boring, but catching up in the car with Maggie made the time go by much quicker. Nebraska, that was supposed a different story. Nebraska was long and flat and often brown and very much the same throughout. I remembered being told by friends who had made the trip out west through

Nebraska that it could be a tedious drive. That would be our drive tomorrow, however. Much to look forward to.

Maggie and I had switched somewhere in the middle of Iowa at a gas station and now that I was behind the wheel, I was getting a little envious that Maggie had zonked out with her head against the window. Her blonde hair bunched up against the glass, a small smile on her face, a cute little button nose, eyelids gently closed. I just found her so pretty. I couldn't help it. She was a pocket-sized woman, little and cute. Looking back and forth, from the long stretch of highway in front of me, over to Maggie, back to the road, back to Maggie, I felt my heart begin to race a little bit. I was feeling something strange sitting there in the driver's seat. It made me nervous.

With her short athletic shorts riding up, I spotted a small triangle of freckles on her inner thigh. Just three freckles, faint and light, with the top of the triangle pointing inwards between her legs. I admit, I felt a little bit like a creeper looking at Maggie like that, but her slight frame was intoxicating. I wanted to reach my hand over and place it on her thigh.

"No," I chastised myself in my head. "No, Dana, that's super weird."

But this wasn't the first time I looked at Maggie and felt this way. If I'm being honest with you, it happened a lot. Maybe, like, *every time* I was with Maggie. I guess that would be accurate. But it always made me feel strange. It always made me feel bad. It always made me feel… confused.

It went all the way back to when we were in college, that

year we were roommates. I had befriended Maggie our freshman year because I thought she was just the coolest girl I'd ever met. She was pretty and tiny — I mean, even tinier back then —and her blonde hair that this pink streak in it. Big geeky glasses back then, too. Hip, really. You know, the artist type. Maggie was so full of life and exuberant, always smiling, always ready for adventure, always working on some impressive project. She most certainly had a lightness about her. Something special. I wanted to condense whatever she had, bottle it, and spray on me every morning so that I could be just like her.

We became friends quickly and just as quickly I found out that Maggie was a lesbian. I have to admit, I was a bit sheltered growing up and I had never met a lesbian before. No, that's not true. I knew *one* girl who was out. And looking back on it, I'm sure I knew other girls who were but I was just a kid, no experience, I never knew who I was looking at. But Maggie, it was no big thing for her. She mentioned her sexuality in passing, grinned and shrugged, and continued on with whatever we were doing. It was inspiring. That frankness drew me in even closer.

Maggie was popular in our circle. The girls liked her because she was hip and trendy and smart, but they also kind of resented her because a lot of the guys liked her despite that she quite openly went after other women. She and I ended up a lot closer than either of us were with the other girls on our floor and by the time our sophomore year rolled around, we decided to be roommates.

Something weird changed within me when Maggie and

I roomed together. I felt some strange feelings that I wasn't familiar with and that inspired some discomfort within me.

I think I can pinpoint it to one specific experience.

Our dorm room door swung open and I watched from our loft, two beds connected to each other hoisted up in the high-ceilinged room, book in my hand, as Maggie strutted in. She had a towel wrapped around her head, another around her body, and she carried a small shower caddy filled with her various bathing products. As she entered the room, she smiled up at me and waved, and then promptly kicked the flip flops off her feet.

It was getting late in the evening, I was reading before bed, and Maggie had just taken a shower post work. If I recall correctly, she worked at the campus art museum on the event nights, sitting at the ticket desk or something like that.

Although I pretended to continue reading my book, I couldn't help but watch Maggie. Pushing her hand into the wrap of her towel, Maggie plucked the terry cloth off of her and delicately removed it, swiftly tossing it up onto a hook that hug off of her closet. She stood there naked, but for the small towel wrapped around her hair, and she opened up her closet to fish through it and find her sleeping clothes. She was beautiful naked. Her body lithe and diminutive, except for the curve of her butt. You might expect a small girl like Maggie to be flat, but she had a plump rear and an ample chest up front. She could almost be described as curvy in her stature. I felt my heart race as I watched Maggie, leaning her arm up against the frame of the closet,

17

absentmindedly bouncing back and forth, leaning on one leg, her behind pumping, the gentle bobbing of one breast visible to me from where I lay.

I felt so naive. I felt naive because, candidly, I was turned on watching Maggie. She was stunning. First Maggie pulled out a tank top from her closet and threaded herself into it, standing there bottomless for a moment, her butt even more pronounced. Then she took a pair of cotton shorts and, insanely enough, she turned toward me to begin putting them on.

That was the first time I'd ever seen a woman with her pubes fully shaved. I knew that it was something some people did, but it felt distant in some way. Like, maybe it was something that just hyper sexual people did. Or movie stars. Or porn stars. I don't know what I thought. But it was so *novel* to me to see Maggie completely hairless and to watch her gingerly slip her small shorts up her thighs.

Then Maggie looked up at me. She had caught me. I think I let out an audible gasp but I'm not sure. Maybe that's just how I felt. But instead of acting like I was weird or something for watching her, Maggie simply smiled at me.

"Are you watching me get dressed?" she said teasingly.

"No," I said. "Maybe."

"Like what you see?"

"Oh stop!" I said, swiftly putting a pillow over my head to block my eyes from looking at my beautiful young room-mate. I heard Maggie laugh. I felt so embarrassed, I felt my heart speedily thumb against my chest.

"It's okay to look," Maggie called up to me. Her voice

had changed. It was more empathetic. In a slow movement, I peeled the pillow off my head and pushed it aside, my eyes peering down from the loft to look at Maggie. She was dressed now, tank top and shorts, standing there with a smile on her face and her hands on her hips.

"I'm sorry," I pouted.

"What were you looking at?" Maggie asked carefully, her visage amiable and accepting.

"I was…" I said, cutting myself off and feeling that familiar embarrassment well up within. I didn't want to say. I felt so dumb.

"C'mon," said Maggie, her grin growing. I think she knew how cute she was and liked the affirmation. It was just us in that room, private, we were great friends. We could be open with one another.

"Your pubes are all shaved off," I intoned bashfully. This gave Maggie a laugh.

"Yeah?" she said through her laugh. Reaching to the elastic of her shorts, Maggie peeled the front fabric down and revealed again her shorn mound. It was shaved so close, it made me think she had just done it in the shower that night. Her flesh was light pink and I could see the line of her pleat splitting down the middle of her. "So they are," Maggie said, looking down at herself.

"It's nice," I cooed.

"Thank you," said Maggie, grinning at me, her head shaking just slightly. "You want to keep looking?" she asked jokingly, still holding her shorts open, hips forward, presenting for me.

"Oh *God*," I moaned. "I feel so embarrassed." I quickly rolled over in bed and looked away. Before I knew it, however, I felt Maggie's small body climb up the loft ladder, the wood frame of the structure moving just slightly as she ascended, until I felt her hands reach out and grab me, rocking me back and forth.

"Don't be embarrassed, Dana," she said through another laugh. Her rocking of my body was gentle and consistent until I rotating once more to face her.

"I didn't mean to look at you," I whispered. "That was weird."

"It's totally okay," said Maggie smiling. With Maggie so close to me, with what had happened, it didn't feel okay. It felt strange and confusing. I had always thought that I was attracted to guys but something deep within me was flush with desire for Maggie. Disconcerting, to say the least. I felt *wrong* in a way, tricked or something, like... why was I feeling like that? That wasn't how I was supposed to feel. This wasn't how I was told things would be.

I smiled weakly back at Maggie, trying to apologize again with my eyes, and she just looked so kind. She really was a great friend. Maggie reached forward and stroked her hand lightly through my hair.

"It's okay, Dana," she said again sweetly. "We're still friends."

"Okay," I affirmed in a murmur, still feeling like my heart might leap out of my chest. Still feeling scared and different and anxious. I almost felt like I could puke, I was so nervous.

My flashback reverie was broken when I heard Maggie mutter something incomprehensible over in the passenger seat. I looked to her, my eyes wide, feeling that very same anxiety I felt all those years ago in our shared dorm room. It was like my feelings time-traveled, a blast from the past, a telemetry of emotion, something stoppered up for years and now uncorked, a flood of awareness rushing over me. Maggie's eyes slowly opened and she caught me looking at her. She smiled.

"Sorry," she said. "I dozed off."

"That's okay," I said, averting my eyes back to the road.

"Are we getting close?"

"Um," I intoned, looking to the little screen suction cupped to the windshield. "The GPS says we should be hitting Omaha in like 45 minutes or so."

"Awesome," said Maggie sleepily. "Thanks for driving, dearie." She had a hugely content smile on her face and after Maggie readjusted herself in the seat, I watched as her eyes once again closed in a smooth and gradual motion. "Let me know when we can see buildings."

"Okay," I said, still feeling those nerves. My hands were shaking on the steering wheel. Something very odd was returning to me, something exciting but intimidating. I didn't know what to make of it. But whatever it was, however I was feeling, I was grateful that this trip was happening. I was grateful that was I going to be spending a few weeks with Maggie, in very close quarters. And that whatever strangeness was bubbling inside of me, I knew would come to some resolution as these days of freedom revealed themselves to us.

———————

"HERE ARE THE INSTRUCTIONS FOR EVERYTHING," said Michael. He was a sharp young man, maybe a decade younger than Maggie and I, dressed well with a nice haircut. Pointing to a piece of paper taped up near the condo's thermostat. "And you'll probably want to keep it cool in here."

"Yeah!" affirmed Maggie. "It's like 100 degrees out there!"

"It's a hot one today," smirked Michael.

"When we left Chicago," said Maggie. "It was in the high 70s. I had no idea it would be so *hot* in Omaha."

"Yeah, it definitely gets like this," he said. "Let's keep moving."

The condo was small but very nice, situated in the Old Market district of Omaha. A nice little downtown area with tons of restaurants, shops, cobblestone streets. Although we were only in Omaha for the night, Maggie tried to pick the hippest place for us to crash. Michael had a great location and great style with his little home. A nice fluffy couch, a big TV hanging on the wall, a guitar in the corner.

"Here's the bedroom," he said, opening up the door to show off a queen sized bed covered in billowing pillows and sheets. Maggie and I looked inside with interest.

"Just one bedroom?" I asked.

"Just one bedroom," replied Michael.

"I guess I could sleep on the couch," I said, looking over to Maggie.

"Don't be silly," she said. "That bed is big enough for both of us."

"Where do *you* sleep?" I asked Michael. He responded with a laugh.

"Is this your first time doing AirBnB?" he asked teasingly.

"It is."

"I go sleep over at my boyfriend's place," he said cheerily. "Whenever someone rents out my condo, I just set everything up and make myself scarce. In fact, I need to get moving shortly to meet him for dinner."

"All right," I said. "Noted. I feel kinda silly about it now." Michael laughed again, as did Maggie.

"C'mon," said Maggie, reaching over to me and pulling at my hand. "Nobody cares."

"So you ladies are only in Omaha for one night?" said Michael, deftly changing the subject to help me out of my social trouble. "What's up with that?"

"We're just passing through," said Maggie. "We're heading out to Boulder."

"Oh, I *love* Boulder," said Michael. "It's a beautiful place. If you love outdoorsy activities, it's heaven."

"We're looking forward to it!" said Maggie. "Right Dana?"

"Absolutely," I said with a smile. I still felt a bit trepidatious about sharing a bed with Maggie. I mean, look, I know there's nothing weird about it, nothing out of the ordinary, just two friends sharing a bed as they pass through town on a road trip, but these feelings brewing up inside of me really gave me pause. I knew that I was totally sexualizing Maggie in my mind, that right there was concerning enough, but I knew that sharing a bed could only make matters worse. It made my stomach ache. But not in the way it aches when you're hungry. Something different. Something anticipatory.

I needed to get my head on straight. I felt like I was swimming in uncharted waters.

"Well... *great!*" said Michael. "I'm going to leave you ladies be. My number's on the sheet by the thermostat. Just text me if you need anything."

"Thanks Michael," said Maggie with a smile.

After a few more pleasantries, Michael handed us the keys and took off, leaving Maggie and I alone there in the condo. We had brought all of our bags inside, feeling that typical Chicago fear of never wanting to leave anything valuable in your car overnight. It didn't seem necessary in Omaha but you could never be sure, I guess. Big city life can do a number on you.

As she leaned over to dig through her duffel bag, Maggie's shorts rode higher up on her butt and I couldn't turn away. The backsides of her thighs were creamy and white and the material of the shorts stretched out over the curve of her rear. I took a deep breath and tried to relax.

"I'm starved," said Maggie, popping back up with her wallet in her hand and grinning at me. "Let's eat!"

We did dinner at a local Mexican restaurant that was totally not like the Mexican restaurants we were used to in

Chicago. It was a strange situation, to be honest. We were also used to Chicago prices and when we ordered the $8 taquitos, we expected a half-dozen tiny fried wraps but instead received a full dozen large flour tortilla monstrosities. Maggie and I laughed about it and sipped from our over-sized margaritas.

When you're on the road, you have no idea what you're going to get. And that's part of the charm. You get so used to things being the way they are in your every day life, the differences you find when you're out of your comfort zone are always new and surprising. Maggie and I laughed about how big the taquitos in Omaha were, there was no way we could have eaten them all, but we loved the experience of the surprise. We loved sharing that moment when the plate was brought out and our expectations were shattered.

We walked around Old Market a little bit after dinner, but we were both admittedly tired from the drive and now a bit dizzy from the margaritas. And yeah, it was still 100 degrees out. We had another 8 hour driving day ahead of us if we wanted to make it to Boulder in two days so we jointly decided to just head back to the rental, have a little more wine, and turn in early.

Together on the couch, in our lounging clothes, Maggie and I each nursed a glass of red wine that Michael had left for us as a gift for staying with him. It was a nice gesture.

"I'm so much happier to be in here than out there in the heat," mused Maggie as she sipped from her glass. "I think I totally sweat through my shirt out there." I laughed and nodded.

"I guess it gets hot in Omaha in the summer," I replied. "And a stomach full of oversized taquitos doesn't help anything."

"Right!" she laughed.

"So…" I said, trying to switch subjects. I had some things on my mind. "What's the deal with Piper?" I can admit to you that I was feeling a bit jealous the more I thought about it all. Piper and Maggie had dated before and it made me wonder what this trip was all about for Maggie. Was it meant to be some rekindling of their former romance? Was I just a tagalong? Even worse, would I be totally forgotten about once we arrived in Boulder?

"She's a cool chick," said Maggie. "She works for this weather research facility there. I think it's called NCAR? I'm not sure *what* she does really. Some sort of science-y weather stuff."

"That's cool," I said. "But… that's not really what I mean."

"What do you mean?"

"Like, what's the deal with you and her?" I said, feeling like I was fumbling through it. It really wasn't my place to ask about it, nor should I care, but it was like I couldn't stop myself. I did care. I was worried.

"*Really?*" said Maggie, laughing, leaning over and setting her wine down on the coffee table. "You jealous or some-thing?" Maggie said this with a fire in her eye.

"No!" I protested with a lie. "C'mon. I'm just, you know, *interested.*"

"Right," said Maggie skeptically. "Piper and I are over

with," she said sweetly, reaching her hand over and petting my thigh as though she were consoling me. This gesture quickened my pulse. "In fact, we hardly even started. We dated for a little while but it was all sex." Maggie said, waving it off. "Relationship-wise, we clashed a bit. It just wasn't happening. But in bed... *phew!*" She dramatically wiped at her brow.

"It was good?" I peeped.

"*Real good*," said Maggie. "That girl has a silver tongue." I'm sure I made a face, scrunching up and looking putting off, which gave Maggie a laugh and probably made her think I was grossed out by the conversation or something. Really I was just nervous and jealous. "I'm sorry," she said, still giggling. "You probably don't want to hear about what lesbians do behind closed doors."

This gave me a pause. I thought about what Maggie said and actually, being honest, I *did* think about it. I thought about it a lot. I took a deep breath, feeling the wine move through me, a boldness welling up inside of me.

"No," I corrected lightly. "I don't mind."

"So you *want* to hear about it?" said Maggie incredulously. Her face was bright and amused. She was definitely having a good time playing with me. "What am I saying? What woman doesn't like to have their pussy licked?"

"At this point I'll take any kind of action I can get," I said, saying this with a hint of trepidation, just trying to lighten up, but also trying to open up as well.

"*Totally!*" called out Maggie through yet another laugh. She was having a blast and this inspired a similar feeling in me. I took another drink from my glass and smiled. Maggie was such a pretty lady. That blonde hair really did it for me, so voluminous and thick. And such a nice, fit little body. I bet she was really tight all over. Looking over at her, I caught a glimpse of her cleavage peeking out from her low cut shirt. I imagined what her breasts must looked like.

"So, I mean, are you gonna ditch me and screw around with Piper while we're in Boulder?" I asked frankly. "Should I anticipate figuring out some things for myself?"

"Dana!" Maggie protested. "C'mon. Really? You think I'd ditch you to screw around with my old fling? No way." With that, Maggie flipped her hand nonchalantly, like I was being crazy for thinking it. "I'd never want you to feel left out."

"I guess all *three* of us could get together," I said brashly, almost blushing into my wine. Maggie offered a huge giggle at my suggestion, reaching to my thigh again and giving it a squeeze.

"You're bad, Dana," she said at the tail end of her laugh. "But I have to admit that *would* be fun. Corrupting the straight girl," Maggie said, devilishness in her eyes, grinning at me. This whole time I could feel my heart racing. The conversation made me vibrate, rife with a sexual tension I hadn't really felt before. I demurred at Maggie's words, looking down, and caught myself staring into her bare creamy white thighs and longing to put my hands on them as she had done so casually to me.

"I'm on vacation," I said with a lackadaisical shrug.

"You're totally on vacation," smiled Maggie, her eyes

meeting mine. We held each other's gaze for an expectant moment. It made me feel nervous and I completely loved it.

"I'm really happy to be free from Paul," I admitted slowly, going for my wine to try to shove something in my mouth. But I couldn't stop myself from talking. "That just never felt right." From Maggie's response, I knew I had said this information differently than I'd said it before.

"Oh really?" said Maggie, biting her lip, offering a slow nod, egging me on to speak a bit more.

"Yeah," I said. "I don't think that was right for me."

"Why'd you do it then?"

"I guess I thought I was... *supposed to*," I admitted. I'd never really said it like that to anyone before. It felt weird coming out but it also felt right. Correct. "What was I? 30 when we met? I don't know. All my friends were getting married."

"Yeah," said Maggie, nodding along with me, trying to figure out what I was saying. I could see in Maggie's face that her brain was working things out. "You know, Dana," she began. "You can always talk to me about whatever it is you're going through. We go way back. You can trust me."

"I know," I said shyly. I wasn't normally such a shy woman but all this stuff was just coming out so fast. I was still feeling strange and confused internally but in a way I felt extremely safe with Maggie. And when you're on vacation, when you're outside of your normal life, some things are easier to accept and just run with.

"Was it just Paul?" she asked cautiously. "Just the wrong *guy?*" Maggie said, really emphasizing that last word.

"Something like that."

"Hmm," Maggie responded. She once again had her wine glass in her hands and she swished around its contents as she contemplated.

"Enough about him," I said, feeling somewhat flustered and trying to change the subject. "That's over with. I'm happy I'm moving on. I don't want to think about that life anymore. This is the start of something brand new for me."

"Right," said Maggie, brightening up once again. "We're going to have a lot of fun on this trip, Dana. I'm totally certain of that." Maggie smiled over at me and I happily returned her expression. She lit up my heart. Maggie was this special beacon to me. With her, I knew everything was going to be all right.

"I'm ready for whatever!" I said, a silly grin on my face.

A BIT later on that night, I had already done my routine and climbed into the big bed all alone, pulling the fluffy blanket up to my neck and getting cozy. In the heat of summer, it's always nice to be in an air conditioned house buried under blankets. Isn't that strange? It's warm outside so we cool it down and then we warm ourselves up again with blankets. It's just... *comfortable*. Lying there in bed, snuggling into the sheets, I listened as Maggie went through her bedtime routine in the bathroom right next door. My heart pumped with excitement, my eyes trained on the door, awaiting her arrival.

I was far too excited to sleep in the same bed as Maggie. I just hoped that it wouldn't keep me up all night.

After a few moments, I heard the light click off in the next room and then watched as Maggie sauntered into the bedroom. She was wearing her tank top, obviously braless, her breasts hanging behind the thin fabric of her top, nipples pointing out and offering a glimpse of their shape. Below, Maggie just had on a pair of pale pink panties. Her blonde hair was pulled up and as she walked further into the room, she removed her glasses and set them on the bedside table. This woman was gorgeous to me. She was a beautiful angel.

"Room for one more?" she asked teasingly. Maggie then yanked at the thick blanket and climbed into bed.

"Of course," I said, smiling, pretending like I was on the precipice of sleep, but eager to feel Maggie's warmth lying next to me.

"We're getting up at, like, 6AM tomorrow," she said. "Is that cool? I really want to get on the road."

"That's cool."

"Good," Maggie said. Reaching over, she flicked the bedside table light off, causing the room to completely go dark. "The alarm on my phone's set."

"Mine too," I said. "Just in case."

"Great," she said. I could feel her smile in her words. "Goodnight Dana."

"Goodnight Maggie," I said.

I felt the sheets and the bed shift as Maggie made herself comfortable, her legs pumping back and forth, her butt grinding down. After a moment, she turned on her side and tried to get comfortable that way. I listened to Maggie's breathing, which at first conveyed that she was still awake and searching for sleep and steadiness. But soon it became methodical and began to slow. I felt the exact opposite. I could feel my heart thumping hard in my chest. I could feel a slight anxiety within me. I was lying so close to her. I thought of her nice round butt underneath those pink panties, really only a foot or so away from me there under the blanket. While Maggie was obviously melting in the exceptionally comfortable memory form mattress underneath us, I was feeling amped up and excited and didn't expect sleep any time soon.

I could smell the sweetness of Maggie's hair, some sort of floral conditioner. It smelled clean and fresh. I imagined pushing my nose into the back of her hair and taking a long, deep breath, trying to inhale Maggie's essence, wanting so badly to be close to her. Right up next to her. I was so damn close. I could just scoot over and I would be there, spooning her. I could slide my arm over her, pull her close, press my palm to her stomach. Hold tight. Oh my God, I couldn't believe I was thinking such things. It was making me wired. I raised my hand up to my breast and felt my heart. It was beating so fast.

Then I imagined reaching my hands out under the sheet and taking hold of the back of Maggie's panties, pawing at the elastic, and pulling them down over her butt. I'd then slip my hands down and take her firm cheeks in my hands, offering a squeeze, my fingertips reaching out to feel the backs of her thighs. Maybe I'd even reach further inside and feel the downiness of her secret fur.

"Stop," I thought to myself. "Don't do this."

But I couldn't help it. The pull to think about Maggie in a sexual way was just too enticing. I'd slip my finger down her crack and underneath her, moving between her legs, offering her furry folds gentle and methodical caresses. That's exactly what I wanted to do. I wanted to feel her wetness in my hand. I wanted to press myself against her small figure and writhe there together in that comfortable bed. The thoughts monopolized my brain. They were so strong, so powerful. One hand down the back of her panties, elastic against my wrist, fondling her as she grew wetter, the other reaching around front and squeezing one of her tits from underneath.

I absently scratched an itch on my inner thigh as I considered this fantasy and as I did this, I felt the side of my hand bump up against my mound, the fabric of my own panties feeling soft against my hand. This accidental touch felt good, so I moved the side of my hand back and forth against my panties, feeling my fleshy lips underneath move along with me. It was all feeling pretty great. There was a subtle wet spot where I had begun leaking from the excitement perpetrated by my mind. I rubbed the wet area in slow circles and sighed aloud, quickly silencing myself as I realized what I was doing. And that yes, Maggie was indeed lying next to me in bed.

I pulled my hand back and scolded myself. What was I doing? Was I crazy? Was I really masturbating over thoughts of my friend, sexualizing her as she slept a foot away from me?

But I couldn't stop. Pressing my palm against myself, I rubbed up and down through the tensile fabric of my underwear, loving the pressure of my hand against my aching flesh underneath. Maggie was totally unaware, sleeping soundly, and I took in another deep breath of the wonderful scent wafting off of her as I continued pleasuring myself.

My legs starting pumping back and forth as I got into it, though I tried to steady them so as to not wake Maggie. My breathing intensified. I was loving it. I imagined Maggie flipping over and sliding her hand between my thighs, helping me along, grabbing at my middle and giving me some tender squeezing and rubbing. The excitement within me doubled. I pinched at my lips through my panties, pulling, yanking, feeling the underside of my panties becoming soaked. I couldn't believe I was doing this and it made me even more excited. I had actually gotten pretty good at silently masturbating in bed while someone slept next to me. A marriage you shouldn't have gotten into will help with that. I don't advise it. But all that practice was definitely coming in handy.

Pulling my hand up, I eagerly pressed it into the elastic band and traversed my fingers downward. I parted my pleat with wanting fingers, sopping up some of my wetness, and guiding it upwards back toward my throbbing bead. As soon as I touched myself there I had to bite my tongue, else I knew I would have called out. It was amazing. I flicked at myself in quick concentric circles, knowing just how to complete my own puzzle, feeling the excitement building up inside of me and the pressure grow.

I leaned my face over and buried my mouth into the pillow. I wanted to be sure I wouldn't make any noise once the moment hit me.

With my thighs squeezed against my wrist, my fingers wetly rubbing, eyes squinted, I let my imagination run wild. I pictured burying my face into Maggie's muff, licking her, tasting her, smelling the aromas of her sex. I wanted to fuck her so bad. I'd always wanted to fuck her. That was something I found difficult to admit to myself in normal everyday life, but easy to concede when I fingered myself and was suffused in sexual appetite. This wasn't the first time I'd masturbated to thoughts of Maggie. That's probably obvious to you.

I thought about going down on her, lapping at her, slipping my finger inside of her and penetrating. I pictured Maggie throwing her head back, moaning, loving my actions, when I suddenly felt my legs begin to judder. My thighs clamped onto my wrist hard and I folded over, whimpering into the pillow, that wonderful orgasmic energy pumping through my body and making my fingers and toes go slightly numb. I loved it. I even laughed a little bit through my whimpers and sighs, sounds hopefully obscured by the pillow. I gently pet myself with wet fingers, each subtle movement giving me another shiver as I came, as I traveled that spectacular sexual voyage.

"Hmm?" I heard Maggie sleepily intone from where she

lay next to me. Fear overtook me, even though I still had the orgasmic chills. Maggie rolled over slightly and hazily opened her eyes, looking at me. As I saw this happening, I made sure to shut my eyes tightly, but not *too* tightly, and feigned sleep. My left foot was still kicking as the remnants of my climax dissipated but up top I was doing my best to pretend like nothing was out of the ordinary. I faked a yawn.

My heart raced. I felt caught. I prayed that Maggie would just turn back over and go to sleep.

"Okay," I heard her say in that same sleepy tone. I felt the bed move slightly, the covers pull, as Maggie returned to her slumber. She hadn't heard a thing. It was just all in her head. Go back to sleep.

Slowly, carefully, I slipped my hand out of my panties and wiped my own wetness onto my t-shirt. I inhaled deliberately and then exhaled just the same. I felt amazing. My panties were moist and sticky now but I didn't mind. I had gotten away with it. It was such a perverted little secret and it burned an intense fire within me. I was ready for even more craziness.

WITH MAGGIE BEHIND THE WHEEL, we drove down the exit ramp and stopped at a stop sign where a road intersected. Farmland all around us. This was Nebraska. Actually, I didn't think it was that bad if you can believe it. Sure, it could be boring, it could be monotonous — and surely *nothing* else in the state was like Omaha — but it was a fine drive. Just flat.

Pulling into the gas station, the only building around us that I could see, Maggie and I were in conversation as she drove up to one of the pumps and shifted the car into park. She killed the engine.

"So I saddled up to the bar," I said. "Because I was tired of waiting for the waitress."

"Wait... what?" said Maggie with a confused look on her face.

"What?" I said, sitting up straight in my seat. "Yeah, I told you, the waitress was taking forever."

"No," said Maggie. "You *what-ed* up to the bar?"

"Saddled," I said.

"Like... you rode a horse?" she asked, unable to suppress her impending laughter. "Like *saddled* the waitress with debt?"

"What?" I said again, a smile creeping on my face. "Is that the wrong word?"

"*Sidled*," said Maggie. She reached over and gripped onto my thigh, giving it a firm squeeze. "You *sidled* up to the bar."

"Oh, *whatever*," I cooed, tossing my hand flippantly. "Maybe the barstools were made out of horse saddles and I *did* actually saddle up at the bar. You don't know."

"You're ridiculous, Dana," she said, still laughing at me. I couldn't help but laugh also. It was infectious.

"Just get the gas," I said, swatting at her hand on my

thigh but secretly loving her touch. "Do you want my credit card?"

"*Yes!*" she said.

"Fine, fine," I replied, fishing through my purse and then handing Maggie my credit card. "You're such a *nut*," I said.

Maggie blew me a kiss, offered a smile, and then flung her door open. I watched as she pushed my card into the pump, removed the nozzle, and pushed it into her tank. She had left the car door open and the car itself offered up a repetitive dinging sound. Reaching over, I pulled the keys from the ignition and dropped them into one of the cup holders.

"Yeah, that was getting annoying," I heard Maggie say, peeking her head in from outside and grinning at me. As the gas pumped into the car, Maggie put a foot up at the bottom of the door, leaning, causing the stretchy cotton skirt she wore to shift up higher on her thigh. Unable to stop myself from peeking in, I saw those same pale pink panties that she wore last night as I watched her crawl into bed. And my heart melted. It all came bubbling back into me. I felt the infatuation grow.

It was almost as if she were doing it on purpose, pumping her leg back and forth as she stood there, showing off what she wore underneath. I couldn't stay silent about it.

"Mags," I said. "I can totally see your panties."

"Oh?" she said, looking down at herself. Taking hold of her skirt like she was going to pull it down over her thighs to obscure what was underneath, she instead flipped it open to give me a better view. She laughed impishly before covering herself back up and taking her foot off the car.

"I didn't say to *fix it*," I said, grinning with a feigned shyness.

"You're lucky I'm wearing *something* under there," said Maggie, quickly looking to the pump to see how far along it was, then darting her eyes back to me. "I've been known to go commando in a skirt."

"I'd like to see that," I said automatically, immediately wondering how in the hell something like that was able to exit my lips. Was I going crazy? I was never that brash, never that forward. I don't know what was happening with me.

"Dana, Dana, Dana," said Maggie slowly. "You're full of surprises."

"I'm on vacation," I said matter-of-factly.

"Right," she said. "A vacation from your normal life. From the life you want everybody to *think* you live."

"What's that supposed to mean?"

"Nothing at all," she said with a knowing smile. "I love that you've still got some spunk in you." Just then, the gas pump clicked and stopped pumping. "And I'm amazed now that at 35, and for all the years we've been friends, you've never before said this kinda stuff. It's... *interesting*," said Maggie, offering me a wink before attending to the gas pump.

My pulse quickened. The conversation was taking a turn and it was definitely exciting, but also a little scary. I wasn't quite sure what I was doing, what I was saying. But it felt...

natural. I was being flirty with Maggie and she was accepting of it. It just felt right. It felt like something that should have happened decades ago.

"Hey, you wanna finger me?" I heard Maggie say, sticking her head back into the car.

"*What?*"

"Do… you… want… to… *switch with me?*" she said, correcting my mishearing. "I can still drive if you're not ready."

"Yeah, I'm not ready," I said, shaking my heard, feeling dizzy. But maybe Maggie *did* say 'finger me.' She was the type of chick to screw with you like that, to make you *feel* like you misheard her but doing the whole thing on purpose. She liked to joke around.

"You got it," she said, climbing back up into the car and positioning herself in the driver seat. It was kind of humorous to see her small figure in charge of the SUV. Whenever I drove, I had to lower the seat down a bit.

"Saddle up," I said to her as Maggie put on her seat belt. Looking over to me, she dramatically rolled her eyes.

"*Please*," she said. "You're incorrect *and* you're a total creep for looking up my skirt." Maggie started the engine and put the car into gear.

"*You're* the creep for flashing me," I said. "I know you got a rise out of it."

"You have no idea what you're talking about." Maggie had a wide smile on her face as her eyes focused on the road, pointing the SUV back toward the highway. We sat there together, both of us feeling pretty good I imagine, as we returned to our drive, still with plenty of Nebraska road ahead of us. We were eager for what Colorado would bring, excited for the new landscape, and enthusiastic for everything that was to come with our trip. It was becoming such a magical experience. I loved every second of it.

"Ah!" squealed Maggie, pointing her finger out toward the impending horizon as I drove. "Mountains!"

"Whoa," I mused, tilting my head slightly to look out of the highest part of the windshield. "Those are definitely some big mountains."

"I can't believe how amazing they are," Maggie said, still gazing out at the majesty of the range in front of us. The highway was nice and smooth, not congested at all, giving us an easy path to our destination. "I mean, you hear about how awesome the Rockies are but... *this?*" She motioned with both hands. "Why do we live in Chicago again?"

"I don't know," I said with a laugh. "You're still navigating, right?"

"Yeah," said Maggie, not paying attention to the GPS or the notes on her phone at all. She was still mesmerized by the landscape.

"I think there's an interchange coming up we need to take to get to Boulder," I said.

"Fine, fine," said Maggie with a sweet grin, looking over at me like she had been caught. Hoisting up her phone, she looked down into it, then back up at the road, to the GPS on the windshield, then once more to the phone. "Yeah," she said finally. "Take this upcoming interchange."

"Thank you," I said. "You may now return to mountain gazing."

But how could I blame her? The scenery was incredible. It was like a different world out here. We were used to the flat plains of the midwest and while rolling green fields can be beautiful in their own right, the mountains definitely had our home beat. I could see why Piper had moved out here from Chicago. If you were into the outdoorsy lifestyle, Colorado was your place.

Something I noticed about Boulder once we arrived was that everything was clean and well taken care of. We drove up around a hill through a neighborhood and things were peaceful. A group of kids roller skied down in the hill in the bike lane. Yeah, roller skies. I'd never seen anything like it before. I guess when there's no snow on the mountain, people still need to get their skiing in somehow. I thought about how idyllic this place was, how it was probably an amazing town to grow up in.

"This is it!" called out Maggie, pointing to a stand of townhouses upcoming on our drive. "Piper said there's a parking lot in the front area that we can park in. She'll give us her pass."

"I'm pulling in," I said. "I am definitely ready to not be driving." Maggie laughed at me.

"I offered to switch back again," she said, wagging a finger at me. "But you wanted to make good time."

"Don't point that thing at me," I said, reaching over and

wrapping my hand around her finger. "We didn't need to make another stop."

"You're going to miss the turn!" Maggie protested, trying to pull her finger back. After a moment, I released her and began my turn into Piper's housing complex.

The grouping of townhouses were designed with a very ski lodge type feel. Wooden and earth toned. The area was surrounded by old growth trees and everything just felt really comforting. A light drizzle of rain had started coming down, but nothing crazy. It was misty and the sun still shone through the clouds above.

Together, Maggie and I hefted our bags up on our shoulders and I reached up, pulled the back door down, and slammed it shut. It was nice to get out of that car. Don't get me wrong, there's an amazing feeling driving long distances on an open road but once you reach your destination, it's a great feeling to plant your feet on solid ground.

"I can't believe you never met Piper before," said Maggie as we walked up toward Piper's townhouse. "She sort of ran in our circle for a while."

"If you recall," I countered. "I pretty much dropped out of that social circle after I started seeing Paul."

"Right," said Maggie absently as she remembered. "I guess that did happen."

"Not my greatest moment," I said. "Very ill-advised."

"Well, *whatever*!" replied Maggie brightly. "That's all in the past. You're here now. Dana's back!"

"Dana's back!" I repeated, smiling over at my friend. Maggie had her glasses folded and stuffed into the neck of her shirt and she had the most wonderful eyes. Vividly blue. Swirling with excitement. Her nose was like a button, facial features petite. I felt myself yearning for her. She drew me in and I couldn't help it. Maggie had a communicable happiness in her surrounding aura.

Reaching the front door, Maggie stepped ahead of me and knocked a few times and then leapt back. She smiled at me and I returned her expression. After a moment of silence, the door swung open and behind it stood Piper. She was incredibly sweet looking, pretty really, a short pixie style haircut, a slim and wiry body, with a hippie punk vibe about her. Piper had on a vintage rock t-shirt, tightly fitted and demonstrating that she had no bra on to support her small chest, with matching tight jeans on below, ripped at the knees. She was barefoot.

"Ladies!" said Piper with glee. She jumped forward and wrapped her arms around Maggie, the two of them hugging tightly. I felt a little jealous for a moment but that quickly subsided. The feeling made me think, though, it made me question what was going on with me and these growing emotions I felt over whatever was between Maggie and I. I just pushed it down and put on a happy face as Piper then approached me and offered me a hug.

"This is Dana," said Maggie, motioning toward me after Piper released me from a hug. "And Dana, this here is Piper."

"I can't believe we never met before," mused Piper as she smiled at me. "How long have you lived in Chicago?"

"Like a decade or so," I admitted.

"And we *never* met? That's crazy!" she said.

"I thought so, too," said Maggie. "But she was involved in this guy and she dropped out."

"Bah," said Piper, waving it off. "I'm glad to meet you now, Dana," she continued on. "You're cute."

"Ha!" belted out Maggie.

"Oh jeez," I blushed.

"You ladies need to get in here," Piper said, moving out of the doorway to let us inside. "Put that stuff down and let's have a beer to celebrate!"

Piper's home was three levels. The top floor was a loft that made up her own bedroom and a small office that looked over a balcony to the main living space, the kitchen, the dining area, a first floor bathroom. And the finished basement had a spare bedroom, the room in which Maggie and I would stay together, as well as her laundry area and a second bathroom. It was a quaint space, enough room for a single person. And like the outside, it had that wooden ski lodge feel. I was really digging it.

"I can't believe the scenery out here," said Maggie, cradling a beer bottle between her hands as she sat cross-legged on an oversized lounge chair in the living room. I sat on a couch while Piper had pulled up this modern minimalist style chair and plunked down in that. I felt all the driving tension easing out of me. I drank from my bottle, sighed, smiled.

"Uh, *yeah*," said Piper. "If you love nature, love hiking, this place is tits."

"Tits," said Maggie, laughing.

"*Titties!*" said Piper, taking another drink. "But no, really, you girls definitely need to do a hike. I recommend Chautauqua. It's right in town."

"Done," said Maggie. "We're game. Right Dana?"

"Absolutely," I smiled. "I'm down for anything. I'm on vacation."

"*Anything?*" said Piper with a devilish smile.

"Within reason," I corrected. Both women laughed at me.

"Well, I hope you two are into weed because it's obvious that we're going to hit up a pot store and check *that* scene out," said Piper.

"How big is it out here?" I asked.

"Oh, it's *big*," she said. "Who'd of thunk it, right?" Maggie laughed and I smiled.

"Hey," I said, waving my hand over at Piper. "Maggie told me you do something weather related? I'm interested. What do you do?"

"Little ol' me?" said Piper with a grin. "I'm a scientist at NCAR. It's, like, literally right down the street from me. I bike to work most days. I work in the Atmospheric Chemistry Observations and Modeling laboratory. ACOM represent!"

"All right," I said, laughing a little bit.

"*Right?*" said Piper, scrunching her face up, still grinning, knowing I probably wasn't following her. "I also do modeling for the Mesoscale and Microscale Meteorology laboratory."

"Piper's a model," Maggie interjected jokingly. This

caused Piper to strike a pose in her chair, lifting her hand up and placing her palm against the back of her head.

"What can I say?" Piper intoned. "I know how to work it."

"Do I dare ask what mesoscale and microscale even mean?" I said.

"You dare," said Piper. "Mesoscale refers to the weather that's happening within a range of a couple hundred kilometers, while microscale is smaller than that. It's all about short-lived atmospheric phenomena smaller than, say, one kilometer."

"Okay," I said. "That makes sense. And you do computer models of that sort of thing?"

"Exactly."

"Piper's a smarty," said Maggie.

"Looks, brains, I mean... I'm definitely blessed," said Piper, ending her humblebrag in a laugh to indicate how silly she thought it all.

"Are you going to be able to hang out with a us a lot while we're here?" asked Maggie.

"Well," said Piper, her jovial tune changing slightly. "Probably not a *ton*. I still have to go to work every day. But I definitely want to go hiking with you ladies and mess around. During the day... you're on your own. There's plenty to do, though, so you won't get bored or anything without me."

"That's fine," said Maggie, looking over at me. "I'm sure we'll find plenty to do."

I smiled at her. I felt really, truly happy to be there in that moment.

———————

MAGGIE and I had just returned to the house from a short hike not too far from NCAR, Piper's research facility. I was freshly showered, lying atop our shared bed on my stomach, wearing khaki shorts and a v-neck, staring down into my phone like it had anything important to tell me. Really I was just waiting for Maggie to get out of the shower. I was so eager to spend time with her. Any time we spent apart, even if it was just for a shower, I felt lonely. I yearned to see her smiling face.

I had definitely loved Boulder so far. It had only been a couple of days but it was an enjoyable place to be. Awesome restaurants, beautiful landscapes, healthy looking people. I could only describe it as yuppie heaven. I imagined you needed a nice chunk of change to live there — it was indeed an expensive place — but if you were well off and liked the finer things, Boulder was your place. I could have easily seen myself settling in there and I admit I gave it some serious thought as I compared it to Chicago.

But maybe I just loved Boulder so much, and this trip, because I had Maggie by my side. Some sort of love by osmosis, if that makes any sense. Maybe I was drawn to this town just as I was feeling drawn to Maggie. I wasn't sure. I didn't know what to think about any of that. It was too confusing for me to work out. It was always confusing until Maggie walked in and showed her smiling face.

And that's what she did. Wearing just a towel, Maggie strutted in from the bathroom down the hall, her wet blonde hair dangling down her back, holding the white terry cloth against her chest as she entered the room. As our eyes caught, Maggie gave me that joyful smile. It warmed me.

"*Hey*," said Maggie in a joking 'valley girl' type tone. "Miss me?"

"Always," I said with a grin.

"I'm already totally achy from that hike," said Maggie, nonchalantly removing her towel to reveal her nakedness underneath. As she reached up to toss the towel over the door, I couldn't help but stare. She had an abundant chest that belied her small frame, a slim stomach with just the slightest hint of a belly, and a bubble butt that jutted out from her lithe legs. Between those legs, downy blonde fur that matched her hair up top. It made me remember of that time in college I'd seen her shaved. The contrast. As Maggie moved, both her chest and her rear subtly bounced with her step.

"Yeah, me too," I said absently, still taking her all in.

Maggie reached down to one of her luggage bags and pulled up a navy colored skirt. Without much fanfare, she stepped into the skirt and pulled it quickly up her legs, situating it at her waist. She turned to me and grinned.

"I'm feeling fresh," she said. "No need for panties tonight." Maggie winked.

I just about melted.

Soon enough, Maggie had threaded her arms into a bra and slipped into a t-shirt, her hair still hanging wetly down her back and imprinting a dark spot on the back of her shirt. Even though I had been pretending to look at my phone as she got dressed, I was indeed watching her surreptitiously. I was mesmerized and couldn't look away. I felt a strange aching in my belly, and it wasn't from the hike. There was something more happening and I was starting to admit it to myself.

I was attracted to Maggie. There was no other way to say it. That's what I felt. Real sexual attraction. It was definitely something I had felt before but maybe I was too stubborn to admit it to myself or it felt too strange. Like, was I really attracted to a female friend of mine? Firstly, I didn't consider myself a lesbian. I didn't think that was who I was. But maybe I was just telling myself a story. I really don't know. It might make sense of things in my life that hadn't made sense up to that point. I mean, the whole marriage thing with Paul that didn't work out. And past boyfriends. It just never felt right. Damn it, had I really suppressed these feelings in a way that totally blinded myself? What in the hell was I doing?

And secondly, Maggie was a *great* friend of mine. How do you tell someone you've known for decades that you, *uh*, find them sexually attractive without making it weird? Yeah, that sounds to me like a recipe for weirdness. I certainly couldn't tell her on this trip, a trip that had put us in multiple bed sharing situations. Oh, and yeah, I also got myself off to thoughts of you in Omaha while you slept next to me. Nothing weird about that. Right Mags?

Through all the happiness I had been feeling, all the expectant jubilation, I suddenly felt let down. Hopeless, really. Like the bottom dropped out of my positive attitude. It made me feel restless, like I wasn't sure what to do or think or say but I knew I had to do all those things somehow. I couldn't believe these feelings were hitting me right then but I also found it difficult to reconcile that it had taken until my 35th year to begin putting these pieces together.

But it made sense. I often looked at other women and felt something different about their beauty. Take for example Piper. When she opened that door for the first time, I found her totally attractive. She was kind of hip, fit, funky, with that short hairdo. But I also found Maggie totally beautiful as well, with her enticing femininity. Other women, too. I remember this one time specifically that Paul and I were out to eat at a restaurant and I couldn't get over how pretty our waitress was. I even told him about it. "Don't you find our waitress super hot?" I asked. Paul agreed. He agreed because he found women attractive. And, well, so did I.

"You okay, chickadee?" asked Maggie, now standing in front of me, hands on her hips. I was still lying on the bed, phone in my hands, and my eyes moved up to her. She was luminescent, happily grinning down at me, floating there like some angel.

"I'm fine," I said nonchalantly. "Yeah, totally fine. Ready to go."

"As soon as Piper gets home we're heading to the weed store," said Maggie with a certain giddiness in her voice. "It's so freakin' *novel*. Just *legally* walking into a store with a bunch of pot and buying it like it's no big thing." I couldn't help but laugh.

"I know," I said. "It kind of blows my mind."

"I don't really know what to expect!" Maggie mused. "Like, is it going to be hidden and secretive. Or will it just be like walking into a liquor store and seeing things out there on the shelves?"

"No idea," I said.

"Are you sure you're okay?" Maggie asked again skeptically. "You seem a little off."

"I'm just peachy," I said, weakly smiling.

———

"I DON'T KNOW how you get anything done out here," remarked Maggie as the three of us walked into the pot store. It was located in an old single story house, quite small, one of those converted stores that had probably been a lot of different things in its time as commercial real estate. I imagined at one time it was a scrapbooking store, maybe an old video rental place, something that probably didn't make too much money and couldn't last long. But now, thanks to the neon sign outside, advertising some sort of makeshift medical logo mixed with a pot leaf, ablaze in bright green, it was quite obvious what this little building had become.

"Just because it's legal out here that doesn't mean I'm stoned all the time," said Piper, laughing at Maggie and giving her a gentle pat on the shoulder. "It's like alcohol, you know? Moderation. Maybe you limit it to the weekends."

"Right," said Maggie. "Makes sense."

"Do you smoke?" Piper asked me.

"Not really," I said. "I mean, in my 20s I did a lot more than I have lately. I'm not against it."

"Dana and I were talking about it," said Maggie. "I think we're both jazzed up by the novelty of this."

"Totally," I said.

"It wears off," said Piper, laughing again.

I try not to be super judgmental but I wouldn't say the clientele at this particular pot shop was the same rich yuppie vibe I got from the rest of my Boulder experience up to this point. There was a guy sitting off to one side who looked pretty straight laced, but then there was this other young guy, sort of a spaz, who was talking loudly about getting stoned and how much he loved it and how excited he was to speak to the *budtender*.

"Yeah, I definitely want some white widow kush but I'll have to talk to the budtender first," he whined aloud to no one in particular, pawing through his scraggly little goatee.

We showed our IDs to the woman at the counter, who then wrote our names down and told us to take a seat. I was a little confused about the whole thing because I guess I had anticipated that we'd just walk in and pull things off the shelf.

"So there are three counters in the back room behind that door," said Piper. "You go up to the counter and tell the *budtender* what you're looking for." Piper said 'budtender' just as the aforementioned dude had said it, giving Maggie and I a wink. "And they tell you what they've got, what you might like, that sort of thing."

"So the stock rotates?" I asked.

"Yep," said Piper. "They often have different weed, different candies and such, chocolates, all that."

"This is exciting!" said Maggie.

"It sort of makes my head spin," I said, giving the other girls a laugh. "I have no idea what to even say!"

"I can just talk if you're uncomfortable," said Piper. She offered me a sweet, understanding smile. She really was a pretty woman. There was something effortless about Piper, something open and liberated and free.

"We'll see how it goes," I confirmed.

Once it was our turn to walk through the door to the back room, I still found myself surprised by the entire experience. The room had wood paneling on the walls, like it hadn't been redecorated since the 80s. There were three counters, as Piper had said, each of them with a glass front that housed many of the different pot edibles and tinctures that the store sold. On top of the counter were glass jars full of weed, each of them labeled with a different name. I had certainly never been in a room with that much marijuana before. At first I was a bit frightened because, hey, this stuff has been illegal for as long as I knew. But I got over that feeling quickly as I saw how casual everyone else was about it.

Piper and Maggie walked up to the counter together and I followed behind. Maggie was obviously excited by it all while I allowed my trepidation to fade. Pot was legal here. This was fine. Cops weren't going to rush in and arrest us all. Times were changing.

"Greetings," said the large man behind the counter. He had long dark hair in a ponytail and a similarly dark beard, braided at the chin, with a loose fitted t-shirt on advertising some corny pot slogan. Okay, I'll tell you. His shirt had a picture of a pot leaf on it and it said *Don't Panic It's Organic*.

"Hello!" said Piper with a grin. "I was in here working with you a few months ago when I had my wisdom teeth out. You sold me those THC patches."

"Yeah," said the man, nodding slowly. "Yeah, I think I remember that. How can I help you today?"

"I'd like some gummies," said Maggie suddenly. "Like sour gummies."

"We've got that," said the man. He turned around in his stool and reached behind him. Returning to us, he placed a white plastic tube on the counter before us. "This here contains 10 assorted flavors of sour gummies, each candy is 10mg of THC, one per dose."

"What's that cost?" asked Piper.

"This tube is $30," he said.

"That is so cheap," remarked Maggie. "I can't believe it."

"Believe it," the guy said.

Both Maggie and Piper went back and forth with the budtender, asking questions, getting his opinion. Honestly, it was almost like speaking to a pharmacist. Will this give me a body high or a head high? What kind of pain relief does this one give? Except, in this case the pharmacist was a pothead with a graphic t-shirt on and he'd probably only woken up an hour ago.

We ended up with a a tube of the gummies as well as some actual pot that Piper wanted for herself, which they call *flower* out in Boulder. I got a kick out of that.

I found the entire experience funny. It was almost like being in a movie. It just didn't seem real. But I enjoyed it all regardless, even if I was ambivalent about the purchase.

Maggie and Piper excitedly gabbed about it on the way back to the car and I just followed behind them with a smile on my face. It felt like we were this tight crew of friends. I felt like I belonged. That wasn't a feeling I'd had very often in the last handful of years. It felt good.

And, just between us, I couldn't stop watching their butts shift up and down as they walked, Maggie in her skirt and Piper in jeans. Maybe that's what was making me smile. They both had really cute butts.

THE THREE OF us sat around Piper's dining room table playing poker and laughing. I found Piper quite hilarious, actually. Jokes just came easily to her. And Maggie, well, it's pretty well established how I was feeling about her. We had all dressed down for the evening, slipping into comfortable clothing so that we could lounge around, have some wine, make merry. I hadn't thought about work, I hadn't thought about my divorce, I hadn't thought of really anything but having fun in almost a week.

Taking up the wine bottle, Maggie leaned forward across the table to fill my glass. As she did this, the front of her top fell open and gave me a look down her shirt. I couldn't take my eyes off of her cleavage. As I starred, Maggie suddenly looked up at me and caught my eyes, as though she knew exactly what I was doing. She smiled acceptingly.

"Piper?" asked Maggie, holding up the bottle, giving me one more knowing glance.

"Fill it," said Piper, pointing down firmly at her glass. Maggie complied and filled Piper's glass.

"Filled," replied Maggie.

"Nom nom nom," intoned Piper, taking the glass up and pretending to eat it instead of drink it.

"I'm terrible at this game," I said, dropping my cards to the table and exchanging them for my glass. "I think I'm much better at drinking wine." I took a long sip. I was beginning to feel buzzed and happy.

"It's true," said Piper. "You aren't very good."

"You're good in other ways," said Maggie, smiling sweetly over to me.

"I've got an idea," said Piper, sitting up straighter in her chair, carefully smoothing her hands out across the wooden table in front of her. "Since you're so bad at this, Dana, we should take one of those pot gummy candies and play strip poker."

I couldn't help myself and released a loud laugh.

"You're kidding," I said, the humor of it quickly fading

into embarrassment. "So *because* I'm bad, we should play strip poker."

"Yeah," said Piper matter-of-factly. "That way, Maggie and I get to see you naked. It sounds like a win-win to me."

"Right," I said. "Win, win." I pointed to each of the women with these words. "Lose," I said, pointing to myself.

"Two out of three ain't bad," said Maggie, grinning impishly.

"While I wouldn't mind seeing either of you in the buff," I said, letting the wine do the talking. "I think my awful card playing abilities would leave me the lone nudist at this table."

"Hmm," said Piper, crossing her arms and sitting back in her chair. I could tell she was working through something in her mind.

"What?" I said.

"Maybe we can come up with a handicap," she said. "Like, instead of a loss meaning you have to remove an article of clothing, you have to have two losses in a row."

"That could work," said Maggie.

"C'mon," I protested, pretending like I wasn't into it but secretly quite taken by the idea of possibly seeing these ladies naked.

"Okay," said Piper. "We'll sweeten the deal. How about the first one who loses, which means the first one totally naked, gets an orgasm from the others."

"All right," I said, very sarcastically. I took a long sip of my wine glass. "I think I'm turning in for the night." The two of them giggled at me.

"I'm telling you, Dana," said Piper. "We eat one of these weed gummies, we're all going to be feeling pretty damn good. I think you'll be whistling a different tune once it kicks in."

"How do you know I would even get off from two women?" I asked under my breath, drinking even more wine. I felt the nerves bubbling inside of me. I was embarrassed, scared almost, but these brazen suggestions from Piper really riled me up. I was totally aroused just from the conversation alone.

"Oh my God," said Piper, her eyes suddenly going wide. "Oh Dana. I thought you were a lesbian."

"Piper!" said Maggie, laughing.

"No really," said Piper, getting serious. "I'm sorry. I was totally under the impression that the whole divorce thing was because you were, you know, *not into dudes.*"

Maggie reached over and gripped onto Piper's arm, giving her a somewhat stern look.

"Piper, just leave her alone."

"I was just having fun," said Piper. "And I was mistakenly under the impression that you were game, Dana. I'm just being an idiot. I really apologize."

There was a silence for a moment, like the air had been sucked out of the room. I felt like I was on the cusp of some monster decision and even though I felt *deep down* that I knew what I wanted, it was difficult to say it aloud. But as I felt the wine absorb into my belly, as I looked across the table at these two gorgeous women, fun and happy and excited and down for whatever, I knew then that I couldn't let this opportunity rush by me. This was the kind of thing that *never* happened to me. Sometimes it's important to take risks and get out of your comfort zone. This was one of those times.

"Get the gummies," I said. As soon as these words came out of my mouth, Piper clapped excitedly and jumped up from her chair, bumping the table in her haste and shaking the wine glasses. She raced across the house in a flurry. I was anxious but smiling.

"THIS IS SO NOT FAIR," I said, feeling super tingly, my eyes looking upwards to the ceiling fan above us, watching it spin, focusing in on it and seeing each individual blade as it cut through the air above. The fan gave me a slight chill as I sat there in my chair, completely topless, my breasts exposed and hanging out, wearing just my sleeping shorts and a pair of panties underneath. "I should have worn socks."

"It's okay, babe," said Maggie, leaning over toward me, grinning happily, her eyes darting from my chest, to my eyes, to my chest, back to my eyes. Her face was lusty, her beautiful blonde hair bouncing with even the most subtle of her movements. "You're beautiful."

"She's right," said Piper, shuffling the deck of cards. "You've got nothing to be ashamed of there." Piper pointed to my chest with the deck of cards in her hand.

"I told you I sucked at this game," I said, shaking my head. But the embarrassment wasn't really there anymore.

After a few moments of being topless, I just relaxed into it. It felt nice, actually. I enjoyed that the two of them were looking at me, inspecting me, perhaps even feeling aroused by my nakedness. Sure, it was probably a bit of courage imbued from the weed and wine but I was happy to feel liberated. I could feel my perspective shifting.

"How about I give you a leg up," said Piper. Reaching down, she took hold of her t-shirt and deftly pulled it up over her head, removing it completely, and dropping it to the floor below. Now Piper was topless too. Her breasts were small but pert, each of them dotted with a tiny firm nipple. She grinned over at me and shook her chest side to side but her breasts barely moved.

"Okay," I said. "That makes me feel a little bit better."

"They're small," said Piper, looking down at herself, giving one of her breasts a tender squeeze. "But they sure are pretty."

"How about you Maggie?" I said, looking over to my friend and offering her a smile. "Are you going to join in?"

"Me?" said Maggie. "If you want to see these ta-tas, you've got to beat my cards." All three of us laughed.

The gummy was really beginning to kick in and I sure felt it. I felt warm and woozy, in a good way, like I didn't have a single worry in the world. We were all laughing together, playing cards, sipping wine, getting inebriated. At times I felt like I was dissolving into the chair, spacing out. But at other times, I was alert and focused on the game, joining in on jokes, slapping the table, being more open and social than I'd been in a really long time. I was coming out of a shell that I didn't even know I was inside of.

Then, suddenly, Piper and Maggie both began smacking the table and hooting, looking over at me with excitement in their eyes. Piper jumped up out of her seat and started dancing, still just topless I might add, while Maggie pointed at me and grinned.

"Do it, do it, do it," Maggie chanted. I laughed as I watched them and then noticed the poker hands laid down at the table. And then I looked down at myself and saw that I was only wearing my panties.

"Oh shit," I said. "Did I just lose?"

"Believe it, sister!" said Piper.

"Ah, whatever!" I said, standing up now from my chair. I took hold of the elastic band of my panties and swiftly pushed them down my thighs, letting them fall to my feet and stepping out of them. "I don't care anymore," I said. "Here I am!" I posed for the women, totally nude now, hands on my hips.

"Turn around!" said Piper, twirling her finger in the air. "I want to see your ass."

"Fine," I said, following her command. I turned around and bent over, showing them my rear. I heard Piper whistle.

"That's a nice ass," she said. "What do you think, Maggie?"

"Really nice ass," said Maggie, laughing along. I wasn't embarrassed at all. In fact, I was having a blast. It felt nice to be adored.

"My only regret," I said, turning back to face them. "Is

that I didn't trim the hedges." Lowering a hand, I ran it through my fur. "Had I known I was going to be standing naked in front of you two, I might have taken better care."

"It's not like it's a 70s bush or anything," admitted Piper, running over to me. Without another word, she lowered her hand and ran it through my pubes just as I'd done. I felt my stomach clench up, a sudden nervousness course through me. But I loved it. I absolutely loved it. "I think it's a nice length."

"Oh my God," I peeped.

"Oops!" said Piper, grinning, and taking her hand off my mound. "I can get a little touchy-feely."

"Hey Piper," said Maggie, she too standing up out of her seat. She had a drunk lusty look in her eyes as she approached us. "Remember what you said about the loser?"

"What did I say about the loser?" said Piper, giving a thoughtful visage as she considered the question.

"The consolidation prize for the loser," said Maggie. "An orgasm."

"Oh boy," I said, feeling a bit of sweat on my brow. The girls looked at me simultaneously and smiled wide.

"Are you down, Dana?" said Piper, waiting for the go ahead with excited eyes. A lot of thoughts ran through my head at that moment, but each one of them was cloudy, confused, uncertain. What stuck out the most, though, was that the possibility Piper was offering was immensely exciting. It was something I'd never experienced before. I'd *never* messed around with another woman, let alone *two* women, and I found both Maggie and Piper so incredibly attractive.

There wasn't much more to it than that. I saw an opportunity for a good time and it would have been silly not to take it.

"I'm down."

"Let's go upstairs," said Piper devilishly. "Grab the wine."

THE THREE OF us sauntered into Piper's lofted bedroom, laughing and joking still, and I cradled my wine glass nervously. Piper carried the bottle and lead the way, her little ass bouncing back and forth with each step, wearing shorts that rode up high on her legs. As we walked, I caught Maggie's eyes looking into mine. I saw a desirous fire in them and it made me feel so comforted, so wanted. And I wanted her. On the one hand, I couldn't believe this was about to happen but on the other it felt awesome. My muscles were relaxed, my mind was eased, I had never felt more excited for a sexual encounter in all my 35 years on this planet.

"Gimme that," said Piper, swiftly removing the glass from my hand. She set it down on the nightstand along with the bottle. Maggie, too, stepped forward and the two glasses down that she had carried.

"Out of the way," said Maggie, bumping her hip against Piper and shifting past her, closer to me. I could tell Maggie was feeling it. Her face was positively dripping with lust. Me, I was feeling stoned and becoming giggly.

Maggie approached me now and slithered her hands around me, dropping them to my backside to caress my naked rear. I felt her palms grip onto my cheeks tightly and my heart just about tore from my chest. I looked down into her eyes and before I knew it, I had leaned my face down to Maggie's level and we had begun kissing.

I sighed softly as I put my hands around Maggie, feeling at the hem of her tank top, slipping my fingers inside of it to feel the softness of her flesh, taking in a deep breath as we kissed. It was magical. Totally ethereal. This was what I wanted. This was what I needed.

"Oh God," I moaned gently as our kiss ended. Between my thighs, I was already warmed and moistening. This was crazy, such a wild ride, but my body was craving it. I felt lightening inside of me.

Piper moved closer to me, standing at my side, and she began kissing me now, passionately and pressured, her hand moving up and offering one of my breasts some firm squeezes and caresses. As she did this, Maggie pressed her lips to my other nipple and began suckling sweetly at it. It was already almost too much to bear but then I felt a hand slip between my legs. Whose hand, I didn't know. But it was a welcomed hand. Its fingers fondled against my aching lips, rubbing over me, causing me to see stars with my eyes closed.

"Who's hand?" I groaned out between kisses against Piper's lips.

"Mine," I heard Maggie say, quickly returning her lips to my nipple.

"It's really nice," I cooed. When I said this, Maggie caressed with an increased fervor, coaxing another deep moan out of me.

My knees were getting weak, my entire body feeling slack as these two beautiful women jointly attended to me. While before I had felt a little angry because of my lack of poker skills, now I was feeling grateful I had lost.

"You're so fucking hot, Dana," I heard Piper say as she fervently kissed me. These words gave me a wonderful ache in my belly.

"Let's lay down," I said. After the words left my mouth, both girls slowed their movements and stepped back.

"I like your style," said Piper.

In the blink of an eye I was lying back on Piper's bed, grinding my butt down into the sheets to get comfortable. I watched as a topless Piper crawled up toward me between my feet, while to my side Maggie was lifting her tank top off over her head, allowing her generous breasts to spill out in a resilient bounce. My heart was racing, the excitement almost too much to withstand. I had two beautiful women coming at me, a belly full of wine, a head messy with marijuana. I just started giggling. I couldn't help it.

Maggie looked at me, saw me laughing, and she herself began laughing.

"What's so funny?" she asked.

"This is awesome," I said. My silliness gave Piper a tickle, who now also busted out laughing.

"Yeah, I'm jealous," said Piper, her palms pressing against my thighs and rubbing back and forth. Her eyes

66

darted down to my middle, obviously focusing in on my ready blossom.

Maggie slithered up next to me and lied down, her arm wrapping around my belly as she scooted up close. Almost immediately our lips met and we resumed kissing. It was spectacular. I felt a yearning for her beyond what I'd ever felt before. Our kisses were eager and desirous and I could taste her sweetness on my tongue. I couldn't help but happily groan as our mouths melded.

"Oh shit," I said in a low whine against Maggie's lips. Piper had lowered herself down to my middle, pressing her lips to my slit, and she had begun kissing me down below with obvious talent. Opening my eyes, I pulled away from Maggie for a moment and looked down to Piper. Her nose was sitting against my bush, her eyes shut, her jaw moving. I could feel the wetness of her lips, the muscled movements of her tongue.

"I bet that feels nice," Maggie whispered, trying to draw my attention back to her with a few soft kisses.

"Fuck," I said with hot breath. "It's amazing." Pipers eyes opened, looked at me, she smiled against my pleat, and then she resumed her lusty work.

As I continued kissing Maggie and feeling Piper's affections between my legs, I felt like a goddess. I felt as though this was what it was like to be Cleopatra. An all-powerful queen who could have anything she wanted. And this is what I would choose. Two beautiful, smart, funny women, just so sexy and perfect, attending to my pleasure. An intoxicated mind, an accepting body. This all added up to pure, unadulterated hedonism. And it was tremendous.

Piper pulled back for a moment and slid a few fingers inside of me, pushing and pulling in a nice steady succession, while leaning in and kissing my wanting bead every so often. I could feel my pulse quicken, my breath begin to outpace me, as Maggie and I leaned together, our foreheads pressed, and our breathing synched up. Looking down, I watched as Maggie's breasts haphazardly swayed as the three of us moved together.

Maggie kissed me one more time before sitting up on the bed, reaching down, and beginning to take off her shorts. She pushed her shorts and panties off in a singular movement, slipping out of them gingerly, until she was presenting her completely naked body for me. Just as I had seen earlier, she was spectacularly beautiful. I couldn't stop myself and I reached my hand out to pet through her bush. Maggie looked down at my hand and laughed.

"You're so lust drunk right now," she remarked. Piper laughed at her and with the hand she had been using to penetrate me, fingers glistening with my own juices, she reached over and petted Maggie's pussy along with me.

"She's in heat," said Piper. "I can tell. This chick is in heat."

"You need to focus on Dana," said Maggie with a grin, batting Piper's hand away from her.

"I'm stoned and I want to come," I said matter-of-factly. Piper laughed at me and immediately pushed her palm against my mound, massaging it up and down. I felt twinkling energy traverse through me. "Mmm," I moaned reflexively.

"Patience," she said through a giggle.

Piper stroked me a few more times before lowering down and returning to using her mouth. As she did this, my head fell back to the pillow and I oozed out a deep moan. Then I felt Maggie toss a leg over me and crawl up further on the bed. Opening my eyes, I saw her small figure above me, breasts hovering, her grinning face looking down at me. As my eyes descended over her body, I saw how close her pinkness was and my mouth began to water.

I wanted to taste her.

"You look pretty from this angle," said Maggie, her hands reaching down and running through my hair. With Piper still eating me out, I flung my hands around Maggie's rear, holding tight, and lifted my neck up slightly so that my lips could meet her slit and I began doing what I felt Piper was doing to me.

I felt a weird energy within me, like I'd just drank a bunch of caffeine or something, as I suckled and licked Maggie's flower. She kept her hands on my head and I felt her hips grind back and forth, my mouth attached to her, as Maggie began panting and sighing along with the increased pleasure. At this point, I was really peaking, feeling just immaculate from the intoxicants, feeling a certain numbness in my toes, yet feeling intensely hot in my middle as Piper slurped.

It was almost as though I were invincible. Have you ever felt that? Have you ever felt so good that you just *knew* that nothing could stop you? That's exactly how I felt. I felt like life was wonderful. Like life was *so fucking wonderful.*

"Yeah," panted Maggie, riding my face. "Yeah." She got this lustful nasty expression that made me want to give her even more. And in my amazingly sparkly awareness, I gripped tighter to Maggie's butt and squeezed. Nice and firm and thick. I felt Piper tickling me with her tongue and I almost forgot to breathe. Without questioning myself or the action, I ran my fingers into Maggie's crack and downward, feeling around until I reached her lips. I immediately and wantonly started to pet her creases.

"Oh God!" I called out quickly and suddenly, my hips squirming, my legs kicking. Piper almost had me there. I was so close I could hardly stand it. I wanted it so badly.

Maggie was gripping to the headboard, focusing on being pleasured, and I was happy to oblige. Her taste was perfection, something along the lines of sweat mixed with a floral fragrance and a tinny aftertaste. I felt her wetness cream down my lips, my chin, my cheeks, the humidity of having my face between Maggie's thighs making me feel sweaty and steamed. I was getting there — oh God! — I was getting there. I rubbed adoringly at Maggie's backside, feeling the downy fur between her crack, I spread my own legs further as Piper locked her lips against my cherry and sucked hard, and my body, now in autopilot, started to shiver and shake.

Underneath Maggie and with Piper still licking me with exalting passion, my hips bucked, my thighs quaked, my feet shivered. My belly was convulsing, sucking in and pushing out with my deep gasps. I muttered obscenities into Maggie's wet lips, still trying to offer my services to her desire, but unable to keep up in any kind of consistent way. I was coming hard and it made me feel like I was floating, like there was no bed underneath me. Rather, the mess of us, three eager and sexy and drunk women, just existed together in this wonderful coalescence of sex. This orgasm felt life changing for me. That may sound like hyperbole but it was nothing but truth. I'd never shook so hard. I couldn't stop myself and nor did I want to.

"Oh fuck," was all I could say as I came down. Opening my eyes for a moment, I saw Maggie looking down at me. Her smile said it all. She treasured me. Her hand moved through my hair, my brow matted with sweat. "Oh fuck," I huffed again.

The rest of that lustful night was a bit of a blur thanks to the intoxicants I had coursing through my veins. But it was a transcendent blur. I loved every moment of it. At one point, we had Piper face down into the pillows, ass up, Maggie behind her with her lips to Piper's pinkness, one hand forward and fondling Piper's small tit. And me, well, I sat on my knees to the side of Piper, rubbing the small of her back adoringly, hand between my own legs pleasuring myself as I watched it all. I admit, I let the sexual beast out of me that night. I had no inhibitions.

We were all taken to the precipice of pleasure that night and each one of us were allowed to experience the other side. It all ended in a sweaty heap of tired flesh, limbs intertwined, lungs demanding oxygen. The last I remember was seeing Maggie's face grinning at me, her cheeks rosy, her blonde hair damp with perspiration, her beautiful chest heaving. We kissed indolently, wanting that connection but also so exhausted from the romp. It was certainly the greatest night of my life. It was so great because it was like having this spiritual epiphany. I knew I would wake up the next morning as a completely different woman.

TWO

*T*he morning following my sexual awakening, I opened my eyes to find myself in bed in the guest room Maggie and I had been sharing since coming to Piper's. I was under the sheets, still nude from the previous night, as was Maggie. The two of us were butted up next to one another, skin sticking together. Maggie had her leg tossed over and tangled into mine. She had a sleepy smile on her face and she looked amazingly happy.

I brought a hand up to her face and slipped a finger into a tendril of Maggie's hair, moving my digit in a slow circle, wrapping it up in her tresses. I wanted to kiss her so badly. I just wanted to lean my face in and kiss her all over, sweetly, tenderly, thankfully.

As thoughts of adoration welled up inside of me, gleefully looking down into Maggie's beautiful face, her blue eyes slowly opened and she caught me gazing at her.

"Morning," she said softly and then yawned like a little kitten.

"Hi," I said sweetly.

"That was a late night," she said. "I'm still exhausted."

"I can't believe I'm not hungover," I remarked, grinning, demurely looking away.

"That's because I made us both chug a huge glass of water before bed," said Maggie, beginning to come to greater consciousness. She stretched an arm up over her head and yawned once again. "Speaking of, I really have to pee."

"Don't leave," I said. Then, lowering my hand under the sheets and slipping my palm between her legs, I cupped her furry floret and offered a tender squeeze. "Just go into my hand."

"You're crazy," Maggie remarked with a tickled laugh. She squirmed a little bit as I touched her. "As much as I love this, I really do have to pee."

Then Maggie kissed me gently and it sent a wonderful shiver coursing through me, coaxing a sigh out of my mouth. She then slipped away from me, tossing the sheet off of her body, and stepped out of bed. I reveled at her naked body as I watched, her copious chest, slim waist, firm butt. It brought so much back to me from the night past. It was almost as though I could taste her creaminess on my lips once again.

Maggie trotted out of the room and down the hall to relieve herself and though I hated to see her go, I loved to watch her leave. Yeah, that's a corny way to put it, but it was true. She had the cutest rump, her cheeks pumping up and down as she made her way out of sight. After a moment, echoing from down the hall, I could hear the sound of Maggie peeing thanks to her leaving the door open. I don't know why I listened so intently. I think it just made me feel incredibly close to her. Like we were sharing something so private and intimate. Like she wasn't ashamed.

I felt real and steady happiness for the first time in a long time as I lay there in bed. I'm sure I had a stupid grin on my face, some joyous look of silly effervescence. I might not have felt so good had Maggie played like the previous night hadn't happened. I might have felt bad. But her kiss and her acceptance of my touches, it made me feel like good things were about to happen to me.

Maggie returned to the bedroom after a few more moments away, leaning her arm against the door frame, smiling at me, modeling her tight little body off for me. I had always thought Maggie was pretty, always pictured what she looked like nude, and seeing her like that was a dream come true. She was probably the most gorgeous woman I'd ever known.

"I'm back," she said sweetly, slowly traipsing back toward the bed until she finally reached it, flopped down, and crawled back up toward me.

"Welcome," I said with an irrepressible smile. Maggie snaked herself back into the sheets so that our flesh could mingle once again.

And then we kissed. It was tremendously romantic. Slow and careful and full of love. It was so enchanting, so eroti-

cally gentle, that I felt my lower half begin to ache and try
to incite a mounting sexual fervor in me.

"Mmm," Maggie sighed as our kiss ended, our noses
touching softly as our hands ran over each other underneath
the sheets. My heart beat hard with love.

"Did last night really happen?" I murmured.

"It did," said Maggie in the same low tone as me.

"It was just…" I began, stopping to try to find the
words. "I never felt so amazing."

"It was *fun*," affirmed Maggie.

"Do you think that things are going to be weird?" I
asked. "I mean, with Piper? And… whatever *this* is," I said,
indicating what was happening between Maggie and I.

"Piper is a strange cookie," said Maggie. "It definitely
won't be weird for her. She's always looking for a crazy sex
romp. You don't have to worry about any weird jealousy or
anything from her."

"Yeah?" I said, mulling it over. "So she's pretty open?"

"Always," admitted Maggie.

"Ugh," I intoned, smacking my hand to my forehead. "I
can't believe everything I did last night." This really set
Maggie off, giving her a big belly laugh.

"You were feeling pretty good," said Maggie. "I don't
blame you."

"Yeah," I said. "But, I don't know… I mean, *you know*."

"You *obviously* wanted to do it," smirked Maggie.

"I did," I agreed. "It felt like something pent up had
been released."

"I'm glad you could let it out of you," said Maggie with

joyous empathy. "Maybe you've been a little repressed for a while, babe."

"Maybe," I said, considering it.

"You like pussy," grinned Maggie, her nose scrunching up, feeling satisfied like she caught me redhanded.

"I might," I said. "I'm willing to give it a try."

"Dana," she started. "I've always had a little teensy crush on you." I couldn't believe what I was hearing. Maggie had a crush on me? Unbelievable. It just didn't make sense.

"Are you for real?" I said. "*I've* always had a little teensy crush on *you*. What happened?"

"You were *straight!*" Maggie countered amid laughter. "I wasn't about to be that predatory chick trying to get you into bed when you totally weren't into it. Though, I admit, it crossed my mind a number of times."

"Well, all that old Dana stuff is just… it's just *behind* me," I said. "I'm open now to just being happy and this… *this*," I emphasized what was happening with Maggie and I. "It's making me really happy."

"I'm so glad," smiled Maggie. She leaned in and planted a kiss on my lips and I eagerly returned it. This kissing lasted a few moments and combining it with the conversation Maggie and I were having, I'd never felt closer to her.

"Maggie," I said after another moment of sweet kissing. "I just want you to know how much I love and care for you," I said this almost having to fight back tears. "I'm sorry that when I was with Paul these last five or whatever years… I'm sorry I neglected our friendship."

"Babe," said Maggie with a grin. "It's nothing. I love

you, too. Our friendship goes way past five years. It means a lot more than all that."

"Thank you," I said in earnest. " Thank you for understanding."

"Of course."

We resumed kissing after this heartfelt exchange and that kissing grew more heated by the moment. Before I knew it, both Maggie and I had begun fondling one another, hands between each other's thighs, teasing the wetness out from our insides. I could feel the arousal both in my middle as well as in my head, the voice in my mind excitedly clamoring for more. The bottom dropped out of it all when I felt a sudden pressure from Maggie's fingers.

"Oh fuck," I called against her lips. Maggie had slipped two fingers inside of me and was thrusting her wrist back and forth, fingering me ardently as the morning sun entered through the small window at the very top of our basement bedroom's walls.

"Mmm," she cooed. "You're already quite wet."

"Yeah," I breathily affirmed, now concentrating on the penetrating of my new lover's hand.

With each measured breath, I felt myself constrict and release Maggie's fingers. My belly tightened, my hips bobbled. I loved the feeling of having Maggie's fingers inside of me, I reveled in how they filled me up. After a few more pumps, she slowly eased them out of my wetness and moved them upwards, settling on my pink dot, and beginning to traverse over it in slow, deliberate circles.

"Okay," I said, my head dropping to Maggie's bare

shoulder, embracing her. I adoringly kissed her shoulder as she stroked me under the sheets.

"Oh boy," said Maggie, moving her hand down once again, spreading her fingers out, and rubbing them over my full and achy lips. "You're totally dripping down here." I felt a single finger press against my pleat and draw upward, collecting my viscous stickiness and smear it around.

"It happens really quickly," I panted.

"I want to see it," peeped Maggie. She had a wicked fire in her eye. Within an instant, Maggie had yanked off the covers and leapt up, crawling down the bed to get a closer view of my middle. I watched as she inspected me, a teasing look on her face, until finally she pressed a single finger against my slit and collected some of my creaminess on her fingertip.

Bringing it to her mouth, she tasted it and made a big production, her lips smacking, a visage of consideration on her face.

"Oh stop," I protested, reaching out and smacking her thigh.

I sat up in bed in a hurry and then rushed over to her, pressing my lips to hers, stealing a kiss, though she couldn't help but laugh. And I absolutely loved this back and forth. It had all the excitement of new love to me. Of novel exploration. Growing comfort. I really felt safe here with Maggie.

"Fine," she said, pulling back from our kiss. "You can taste me." Plopping back on the bed, arms braced behind her small figure, Maggie spread her legs and offered herself up to me. The blonde fur of her mound was so appetizing to me. I could see the subtleness of her crease, the light hair drawing in toward it. It was an impeccable example of womanly sex. Such a perfect pussy.

Looking up to Maggie's face, catching her watching me, I let a smile grow over my lips.

Pressing my palm against her slim stomach, I leaned in and delicately pursed my lips against her softness. I felt the prickles against my lips, inspiring me to kiss deeper. And so I did. I buried my mouth into her sweet slit and parted her lips with mine. Maggie immediately began moaning slowly and rather than continuing to brace herself up, she fell back onto the bed and widened her legs further, ready for my attention.

Right under Maggie's belly there was a gentle line in her skin, and I adoringly ran my thumb back and forth over it as I mouthed into her blossom. I grew intoxicated from her flavor, my own arousal mounting as I tasted her moistness and felt it drip onto my chin. The subtle perfume of sweaty sex wafted up and I deeply breathed it in. Maggie's botanic musk emboldened me to suck firmer against her.

"I'm gonna fuck you so hard," mused Maggie, drunk with lust. She had the sexiest pillow talk. I felt her hand move to my head and begin threading her fingers into my hair. "I'll do whatever you want," she said.

Releasing my tongue, I moved it upwards along her pleat and felt her lips part to either side. Maggie emitted a low whine as I did this, making her pleasure known. Focusing my licking on her little bead, I brought my fingers up and started prodding at her until I was able to enter her with a single digit. I felt inside of her, my fingertip touching over her soft inner ridges, then drawing it almost back out again, leaving just the end of my finger inside and applying pressure to the base of her bloom.

Next, I removed my fingertip completely and pulled it downward, bringing with it some of Maggie's own juice. Perhaps I was a little overeager but I just didn't care. With my lips against her cherry, slurping and licking and adoring her womanhood, I pressed my finger into Maggie's cheeks and offered her rear a firm touch.

"That's nice," Maggie cooed. "I'll really like that." She gripped harder against my hair, pulling at it. But I didn't mind. I loved it, actually.

I increased the pressure on her backside, rubbing the tiny folds back and forth with a wet firmness, while I buzzed my lips against her in front. I felt a shiver in Maggie's body, starting in her hips and then moving down her thighs. She was gyrating like she was cold, but the noises coming from her mouth indicated just how hot she was. This all made me redouble my efforts and as I did, I could tell Maggie was positively enamored by what I was doing to her.

"I'm really close," she intoned between moans. "Oh God, *really* close."

With my finger on her rear, I could feel her moving in time with her breathing, opening up just the slightest bit as I felt around her rim and explored. But just as I was getting the nerve to prod further, Maggie cried out with a squeal and her top half folded upwards, her lower half beginning to quiver with vigor. Her body juddered and she groaned and I just kept sucking her. I could feel her tiny kernel with my tongue.

"Shit!" Maggie called out, her palm slapping hard against the bed a few times. She gritted her teeth and writhed, her butt grinding down into the sheets. I got the message and pulled back from her, letting the smile widen on my lips as I watched her come.

Her middle was totally glistening with dampness, a steamy mixture of my saliva and her sweet nectar. Raising my hand, I wiped at my mouth with my palm and took a deep breath, satisfied with my work below. Maggie kicked her leg out a few times and she lowered both hands to just below her navel, tenderly caressing herself, fingertips running through the very top of her pubic fur.

After a few moments more, Maggie opened her eyes wide and looked at me. She was ecstatic. And this look enhanced my sense of accomplishment.

"I'm going to hire you to do that all the fucking time," she said to me, searching for her breath. "Oh my God, it's so throbby." Maggie's hand lowered to her pussy and she stroked against herself in an effort to console whatever soreness was presented.

Soon I was lying next to Maggie, our bodies cradled together, and I pressed my fingers against her mound to feel her wet and matted fur, lovingly caressing her as she came down from her orgasmic high. I kissed the side of Maggie's face and she sighed, smiling happily.

"This trip just got a lot more interesting," Maggie said. And I agreed.

"Coffee?" asked Piper with a smile, holding a stainless steel French press over the empty mug in front of me. Maggie and I sat next to each other at the dining room table as Piper, dressed in black work pants and a white button-down shirt, served us breakfast.

"Of course," I said. "I could use it."

"Late night," said Maggie with a playful grin.

"*Yeah!*" affirmed Piper, releasing a short laugh.

I think we were all a little bit woozy from the previous night's romp. I know I was. And I could read it on the faces of the other two ladies. Although I felt a bit weird about what happened between us, I couldn't deny how great it made me feel. Looking over at Maggie, her lovely pale visage, blonde locks haphazardly draped over her shoulders, I felt like this was right. Whatever was happening, whatever happened between me and Maggie and Piper, that's what was supposed to happen for me. It felt... *natural.*

"You girls are lucky," said Piper, pouring herself a cup of coffee after filling both Maggie and I up. She sat down and gingerly took a croissant from a plate in the middle of the table. "I have to go to work today and you've got the day to yourselves."

"You could call in sick," said Maggie. "Just call in and come with us to Rocky Mountain National Park."

"I *wish*," she said, her eyes shooting upwards, her head shaking back and forth. "We're doing this test today that I need to be present for. Even if I'm hungover and stupid, I still need to be there. Sometimes it sucks to be in charge of such things." Piper laughed at herself and took a sip of coffee.

Under the table I felt Maggie slip her foot against my ankle, bare skin to bare skin, and rub her toes up and down at a leisurely pace. I looked over to her and smiled. She smiled back.

"Can I bring something up?" I said, looking back and forth between the two of them. "Just something that's on my mind?"

"Shoot," said Piper, blowing on her coffee and then taking another drink.

"Last night?" I said, offering a shrug and wide eyes. Maggie rubbed her foot firmer against my ankle.

"Yeah?" said Piper. "Pretty fun, huh?"

"Well, yes," I admitted. "It was... *really fun*." I thought about it and tried to find my words. "But, you know, also confusing."

"Ah," said Piper with a smile, looking over to Maggie and offering a wink. "Yeah, I get that."

"Do you have any questions, Dana?" asked Maggie tenderly. I could really feel the empathy from her. It was comforting.

"Many," I said. "Well, I *think* many..."

"Well, *first*," began Piper. "I think you two are both babes and you're totally grand but I'm sort of a lone wolf," she said. "And Maggie and I have already been down that road."

"It doesn't work," said Maggie with a knowing smile.

"Right," said Piper. "When Maggie and I were in a relationship, we were at each other's throats. We work much better as *just friends*." Piper smiled sweetly over at Maggie.

"Okay," I said, still trying to put things together. "So that was just... *fun?*"

"Just fun," admitted Piper with a single nod. "And I'm *always* down for some fun." She laughed.

"I know things might feel a bit confusing," said Maggie, reaching her hand over and placing it atop mine to comfort me. "Especially because of what's been going on in your life."

"Oh yeah," said Piper, now remembering my situation. "I guess I totally spaced on that. I'm sorry, babe," she said to me. "But maybe this was, you know, for the best...?"

"I would say, Dana, you should just... go with it," said Maggie. "Maybe this is why things never felt right with Paul."

"Yeah," I said, releasing a deep sigh. I thought about it and perhaps Maggie was right. Honestly, having sex with a man was never something pleasurable to me on an intrinsic level. Of course, I'd had sexual encounters with men before that felt good but that was usually because I was getting played with or eaten out or something like that. Penetration, on the other hand, always made me feel a little sick to my stomach. I could never explain it. It was kind of repulsive to me.

But that night with Maggie and Piper, my inhibitions gone thanks to the concoction of intoxicants, just letting myself go and enjoying the moment with two pretty women, now that felt right. That made me happy. That made me more sexually fulfilled than I could ever remember being.

"If you liked it," Piper said. "But you also like men… well, maybe you're bi." Piper shrugged.

"Maybe," I said.

"This might be too much," said Maggie, trying to cool Piper down.

"No," I countered. "No, this is good. I think I need this."

"Okay," said Maggie offering a reassured smile. Again, I felt her foot run up and down my bare leg.

"Do you like *the ladies*?" said Piper, eyes darting over to me. "I mean, how have you felt about chicks over the course of your life?"

"I mean, I've always found women beautiful," I said. "But I thought that was just something *everyone* felt, men and women and everything in-between. Women are just beautiful, right?"

"Well *I* think so," said Piper. "And I know Maggie thinks so. *Everyone* else? I don't know."

"Have you ever fantasized about another woman?" said Maggie. "If that's embarrassing to answer, you don't have to."

"No," I said. "It's fine. I think that, yeah, I have fantasized about another woman." My heart was pounding and I was feeling nervous by all this, but it felt like it was something I needed to talk about it. Like it was something that had been inside for so long and it was finally getting its time in the sun. Of course I had been fantasizing about Maggie, but another woman popped into my brain.

"Who?" said Piper. Although she was obviously a teasing and playful instigator, I could tell that her demeanor was softening as I opened up.

"When I was in college," I started. "I had this communications class and one of the teaching assistants was this girl Lorna. She was just *so pretty*," I said, exhaling as I reminisced. "It was a huge class, you know? One of those lectures with like 300 people enrolled?"

"Mm hmm," said Piper, nodding knowingly.

"And you never interacted with the professor specifically. He told you to talk to one of the TAs if you had any problems," I said. It was all flooding back to me now and I was getting more and more eager to let it out. "I didn't have any problems except that I wanted to talk to Lorna. There was just something magnetic about her."

"What did she look like?" asked Maggie tenderly.

"She was a brunette," I said. "Her hair was long and straight. She was curvy in all the right places," I said with an embarrassed grin, looking down and feeling a bit silly. "That's to say she had really nice tits."

"Of course," said Piper with a grin. "I love tits."

"Shh," said Maggie, putting her finger to her lips in Piper's direction.

"But just... I don't know," I continued. "I felt *physically* drawn to her. Like I wanted to be close to her. I would go up to her after class and ask questions. I went to her office hours a couple of times..."

"I think we've all been there," said Maggie.

"Totally," affirmed Piper.

"I don't think she knew that I was just engaging her because I was attracted to her," I assayed. "Or, you know, maybe she did know and it made her feel uncomfortable that I was coming to see her all the time. I don't know." I smiled to myself and shook my head.

"Or maybe she was into it too and you totally missed your shot with her!" said Piper. "Maybe she was feeling it too."

"Ha, *right*," I said. "Maybe."

"Did you ever say anything to her?" asked Maggie. "Like, did you ever try to get together with her?"

"No," I mourned. "I mean, I was just so embarrassed for feeling like I did. I was secretive about it all. Like, *c'mon*, you and I were friends," I said, pointing to Maggie. "I totally could have talked to you. But I just felt… that wasn't me. I wasn't attracted to girls. You know? It was really confusing."

"I know," said Maggie, consoling me by running her palm over the back of my hand.

"God, I wish you would have said something to that chick," said Piper. "I love a story that ends with two women jumping into bed." I couldn't help but laugh at her. She was such a bright and lively woman.

"Well," I went on. "I guess it's fine for me to tell you that I masturbated over Lorna a bunch of times."

"Now *that's* what I'm talking about," said Piper. The three of us laughed together.

"I always felt a little bit of shame about it after the fact," I said. "But that certainly didn't stop me from continuing to do it."

"Dana," said Piper matter-of-factly. "I am *so* glad we could have this conversation. I want you to forget all that past shame or feelings of regret or whatever amalgamation of weirdness you've got brewing inside. Just move forward and be *you*. Cool?"

"Cool," I said with a smile, feeling so much better about myself. I'd never admitted my feelings for Lorna to anyone before. It was like I was ten times lighter. It was as though I no longer felt as stifled.

"I think you're going to be so much happier," said Maggie, her eyes meeting with mine. Something was going on between her and I and it was really doing a number on my heart. My brain suddenly jolted back to our bedroom fun that morning and I felt a little tingle in the pit of my stomach.

"I think so, too," I cooed.

"This has been highly productive," said Piper, now standing up from the table. "But I have some microclimate simulation models to run and interpret. The weather waits for no woman."

"Thank you, Piper," I said in earnest, looking up to her.

"You got it, girl," she said. "You two have fun at Rocky Mountain today. I'm totally jealous. Check out Bear Lake and take Trail Ridge Road up as far as you can stand. At least to Forest Canyon. There's probably still a lot of snow up there right now."

"Even at this time of year?" asked Maggie suspiciously. "Are you kidding?"

"Nope," said Piper. "We had a really late snow near the

end of winter this year. And up in the mountains it'll really stick around."

"Wow," I mused.

"All right," said Piper. "Do your thing. Text me if you have any questions. And Dana," she said, looking over to me. "Just enjoy, okay?"

"Okay," I said, smiling.

"Off to work!" said Piper, sticking her finger up into the air.

"Oh!" called out Maggie, her hands gripping tightly to the wheel of her SUV. "My eyes are watering so bad."

"Really?" I asked, looking over to her with concern. "Are you gonna make it? Should we stop?"

"I can keep going," she said. "The pressure up here is crazy."

We had been ascending Trail Ridge Road in Rocky Mountain National Park, walls of snow packed high on either side of us, sometimes coming upon a ledge that offered us a steep drop off. Neither of us had ever been this high up in altitude before, apart from an airplane obviously, and it was just a wild experience. I could feel a subtle anxiety within me every time we drove by a ledge and Maggie was feeling the pressure in her eyes. But we were both determined to make it up as high as we could go.

Reaching over, I gently placed my hand on Maggie's thigh and offered her support.

"We're going to stop at Forest Canyon Overlook," said Maggie, pointing toward a sign by the side the road. As she said this, I noticed a steam of water in the gutter near the wall of snow on Maggie's side of the road. The snow, while at least five or six feet high, was beginning to melt. The road had thankfully been plowed but I had a sudden worry that the snow could possibly fall to the road and obstruct our passage.

"Okay," I affirmed, nodding. "I'm fine with stopping soon. I'm feeling this weird nervousness anyway being up so high."

After a few more minutes of driving, we came upon a small parking lot off to the side with about a dozen cars parked in it. People were ambling around the area, walking up a pathway that seemed to reach out into oblivion. Maggie swiftly pulled the car into a parking spot and shut off the engine.

"My *God*," she said, removing her sunglasses and wiping at her eyes with the bottom of her t-shirt. As she did this, Maggie exposed her slender belly, showing me her cute little navel. I couldn't stop myself from looking at her stomach as she blotted the tears from her eyes. Dropping her shirt, Maggie blinked a few times dramatically, widened her eyes, and then replaced her sunglasses.

"You okay?" I said.

"I'm better now that we're parked," she said.

Stepping out of the car, I was blown away by how cold it was. In our ascension up the mountain, we must have dropped 30 degrees Fahrenheit from where we had started at the base. Our drive to the Park had been warm, definitely in the 80s. But up here in the mountains, the thermometer in the car's console told us we were now in the low 50s.

"I guess we shouldn't have worn shorts up here!" remarked Maggie with a laugh.

"I don't think anybody was really ready," I replied, motioning out to the other people around us, pretty much every one of them dressed in their summer clothing. A girl in her 20s ran by us wearing a short skirt on bottom and a thick hoodie up top.

"Do you see that?" said Maggie, looking across the road into a craggy mount. She pointed and I tried to follow her finger. "What *is* that?"

Off in the distance we saw a little creature. I wasn't sure what it was. There were actually a handful of these animals. I tried to figure out what they were when suddenly Maggie spoke up.

"Marmots," she said. "I think that's what they are."

"They look like gophers or something."

"Yeah," she said. "Something."

"Do you notice that there are, like, no trees up here?" I said. "On the drive up, there were trees along the road. But look," I said, motioning out to the landscape with both hands. "Nothing."

"Yeah," said Maggie, walking up to a sign. I followed behind her but she started reading before I got there. "Oh!" she called out. "This is the tundra. We're so high up, trees can't even grow up here."

"Maybe this is too far up for people to be," I said

jokingly. Maggie looked up at me and smiled. "We're kind of giving the middle finger to nature by coming up this far."

"Right!" she said, laughing. "Let's stick the finger up higher!" Maggie reached over and grabbed my hand, pulling me along with her as she broke for the cordoned off pathway toward the cliff's edge.

We were surrounded by just massive snowcapped mountains. It was like a postcard or something, not a place you're used to seeing in reality. Mountains towered over us, even though we were already up over 11000 feet in elevation as one of the nearby signs read. It was hard to believe. But as I held Maggie's hand and we sauntered around together, I felt excited for all the new adventures coming my way.

"Wow," mused Maggie as we looked over the edge of the overlook. The drop down was impossible to comprehend. What would happen if you fell? Would you ever *stop* falling? It made me feel a tinge of anxiety and I squeezed harder onto Maggie's hand.

"That's *crazy*," I said, looking down. "Is my palm sweating?" I offered another squeeze to Maggie's hand and pulled our hands up together.

"No," she said curtly with a grin.

The area was bustling with other tourists, moseying up next to us, snapping photos, peering over the mountain cliff usually just for a quick moment before stepping away. It was difficult to breathe that far up or maybe it was just the view that was breathtaking. Either way, the excitement of it all made me feel even closer to my friend. It made me feel enthusiastically happy.

It also made me feel intensely introspective. Being faced with the imminent pitch of that cliff, it gave me a new reverence for nature. For this nature all around us. For my own nature. The mountain *just was*. It didn't have to make a fuss over anything. You had to take it or leave it. And I could see that life should be the same for me. I had been fighting my own feelings for far too long. Why would I do that? Why would I make myself unhappy, why would I deny myself? It felt so silly as I looked over the edge. It felt so pointless.

After a bit more time admiring the majesty of these wonderful mountains, Maggie and I made our way back toward the car. With the driver side door open, Maggie sat sideways in the seat, flip-flopped feet propped up on the frame, meticulously unwrapping a granola bar and taking a bite out of it. Her sunglasses were pushed up her forehead, threaded into her hair, her blue eyes wild and bright. I leaned against the door, hand up on top of it, as I watched her.

"Want some?" she asked, holding the granola bar in my direction. I smiled and shook my head. "Okay," Maggie said with a shrug, taking another bite.

"Hey," I said, absently dropping my hand to Maggie's bare knee and leaving it there.

"Hi," she said smiling.

"Our talk this morning with Piper," I said. "About me. I've been thinking about it all."

"That's great," said Maggie. I could see real happiness in her face.

"I've felt so weird for so long," I said. "Sometimes I'd

look in the mirror and say to myself, 'Dana, what are you doing?' You know what I mean?"

"Of course."

"I don't know," I went on, inhaling a lungful of that cold mountain air. Then I exhaled in a sigh. "I don't know why I spent so much time in hiding from myself."

"Do you think it's because your parents wouldn't accept that you were different?" Maggie offered, fishing around for reasons. "Maybe religious crap?"

"Maybe," I said, thinking about it. "But maybe... maybe it's more about my grandmother," I considered. After I said it, things started to open up to me. "You know, she's the total matriarch of my family. Really opinionated lady. Well... not so much anymore."

"Why not?" Maggie said softly.

"She's in Hospice," I said. "I mean, she's out of it. She doesn't have much longer."

"I'm so sorry, Dana," said Maggie, reaching out for my hand. We threaded our fingers together.

"*She's* the hyper religious one," I said. "And she had always been really controlling of the entire family. It wasn't until she fell ill that I felt like I could divorce Paul."

"Really?" said Maggie. "I had no idea."

"Oh *yeah*," I said. "God... she totally would have *shunned* me if she was aware I got a divorce. Ugh," I groaned, shaking my head. "Such garbage."

"What about if you were a lesbian?"

"Probably *worse*," I admitted.

"And how's your family now?" she asked.

95

"I think everything is a bit... lighter," I said. "Now it's just, 'let's take care of Granny' or we go see her, talk to her for about half an hour, try to make her feel good, and then go. It's stressful in a different way, but definitely that sort of domineering feeling we've had for a long time, that's dissipated."

"I think that happens a lot," said Maggie. "You know, whoever you all feel is *in charge* of the family in some way, you don't want to offend them or rock the boat or anything like that. But then when they're gone — or, well, *almost gone* in your case — everybody else can finally relax and do the things they really want to do without fear that the family is going to turn against them."

"Yeah," I said, letting a smile creep onto my face. I absentmindedly played with Maggie's fingers.

"You okay?" she asked. I lifted my head up and our eyes met. Her beauty made me feel skittish. We had so much history together, we went back so far as friends, but I felt like a new chapter was being written in our story and I just wanted to skip ahead to see how it might end. Or truly begin.

"I'm feeling so great, Maggie," I said. "Thanks for letting me tag along on this trip. I mean, it's definitely opening my eyes."

"*Yeah!*" she laughed.

"I had a fucking threeway with two women," I said in a frenetic hush. "That's insane to me."

"We have a lot more time to spend together," said Maggie. She pulled at my hand and I collapsed into her, wrapping my arms around her in a tight hug. Maggie embraced me as well, not just with her arms, but with her legs. I could feel her flip-flops against the back of my thighs.

My face was buried into her hair and I took a long whiff of it, ending in a joyous sigh. Maggie smelled freshly botanical. And in my arms, hugging together tightly, her small frame felt like a perfect fit.

"I'm glad that experience got me out of my shell," I murmured. "It could have been weird but it so wasn't. It was just what I needed."

With Maggie sitting there, me standing, the two of us locked in an embrace, things had never felt more comfortable for me. I felt like I was finally able to be myself and I was accepted for it. I wasn't hiding anymore. I was like a debutante coming out for the very first time, showing my happy face, letting the world know who I was. The feeling of freedom was addicting.

THERE WAS something unspoken happening between Maggie and I, something putting us on the same page, and it came as no surprise to either of us when we jointly decided to cut our time staying at Piper's a bit short. Piper was sad, yet understanding. We had told her we were eager to keep driving west to see what was out there for us and although she entreated us to stay, I knew she could see something between Maggie and I when we looked into each other's eyes. It didn't need to be acknowledged. We could all feel it.

"It feels like your time in Boulder was so *short*," said Piper, almost pouting, as I slammed shut the rear door of Maggie's SUV. We had packed all our things up and were just about ready to take off.

"Maybe we'll stop back through on our way home," said Maggie with a smile. Stepping forward, she wrapped her arms around Piper and the two hugged deeply.

"You're totally welcome to," said Piper. After Maggie released her, I stepped forward to hug Piper as well.

"Thanks for everything," I said. "It's really been life-changing out here."

"I can only imagine," said Piper with a laugh. She then kissed the side of my head with an exaggerated sound. "Mwah!"

"It really is magical," I said, releasing Piper and standing back. "Colorado is such a beautiful place."

"Yeah, I don't think I could ever live anywhere else," said Piper with a smile. "This is my home now."

"It's going to be *real* hard to go back to Chicago eventually," said Maggie.

"You don't ever have to go back," said Piper assertively. "You ladies could both move out here and we could totally take this town by storm."

"There's the whole job thing…" I said, rolling my eyes back and flicking my wrist.

"Oh yeah," said Piper. "You couldn't find jobs out here or anything."

"Let's get away from this Colorado evangelist," said Maggie with a wry grin, slinking up behind me and gripping onto my shirt. She peeked her face around me and stuck her tongue out at Piper.

"Come to the Promised Land!" said Piper, waving her arm out in front of her. "All are welcome!"

"Run Dana!" said Maggie, pinching me from behind and giving me a tickle. I squirmed and laughed. "She's going to convert us!"

"I could be convinced to stay," I said with a smile.

"Nah," said Piper. "Get your asses out of here. I'm done with you both."

We all laughed together, offered up more hugs, and then Maggie and I climbed up into the car, waving at Piper as we drove off.

I guess that's how it works when you're on a road trip. Things just move quickly. You make a stop, hang out, have a bit of fun, and then pull up stakes to move on to your next destination. I was happy to have met Piper. She was certainly a character, a good person, and undeniably sexy. As we drove off into the new morning, I recalled back to that lusty night the three of us had. It put a smile on my face. I wouldn't forget Piper very soon.

Sipping hot coffee out of a paper cup, I basked in the comfortable silence as Maggie drove us down I-70 across Colorado and toward our next stop. Salt Lake City, Utah. I didn't know what to expect out in Salt Lake City. It seemed like a place people often talked about, but it felt so nebulous. Apart from the Mormon thing, I had no real knowledge of it. Maggie had told me there was some killer hiking in the surrounding area so I took her word and opened up to whatever might happen next. I didn't really feel too attached to the past or the future. Right now was feeling pretty good as it was.

The scenery grew even more beautiful than I would have through along our drive. The highway took us through some of the ski resort mountain towns and eventually up the steep slope over the continental divide. If you're unfamiliar with the continental divide, it's the mountainous region in the States that separates the watersheds. West of the continental divide, where we were headed, the water drains toward the Pacific. East of the divide, water drains toward the Atlantic.

"Hold on to your butt," said Maggie as we surmounted the highest point of the range and began our descent.

"That sign says to not ride your brake," I said, looking out the window and pointing. "Why's that?"

"I think that's for the big rigs," said Maggie. "If they ride their brakes, they can overheat and give out."

"Ah," I intoned. "Well, let's not let that happen to us."

"It's really hard not to keep your foot on the brake," mused Maggie as she drove. "This road is super steep."

"Drive us to safety, Mags," I said, tenderly petting her leg. "Drive us to safety."

She smiled at me and blew me a kiss.

Before setting off on this trip I had a lot on my mind. I didn't quite know what I was going to do next. The divorce was final and I was on my own. I was happy about that, definitely, but at the same time it made me feel lost. Work was... whatever. I did account management at a financial services firm. It wasn't very exciting, though it was stable enough. It didn't seem like the right fit, ultimately, though. I was envious of Maggie who got to do something she loved, teaching fashion at an art school. I mean, how cool is that? I felt boring in comparison. I just wasn't sure what direction I was actually headed in.

But now, as we drove, I was comfortable in the uncertainty. I didn't dwell on it. I felt that, at my age, I still had a lot of life ahead of me, a lot of opportunity to define myself and figure out what made me happy. And I felt that was beginning with Maggie. With our relationship. With what was becoming of us.

I hadn't allowed myself to imagine what it would be like to actually *be* with another woman in a long time. I tried to stuff those feelings down. I tried to deny them. But I didn't have to hide anymore. I knew that the road ahead of me could be tough, there could be some hurdles, but I guess that's what life's all about. If we didn't have to fight for what we wanted, would we even want anything at all?

"Boop!" said Maggie, gingerly poking her finger into my side. I laughed, looked down, smiled. She looked at me and grinned and then returned her eyes to the road.

This was like a dream come true.

N<small>OW IN THE</small> barren desert of Utah, the mountains decidedly browner than those in Colorado, we drove north to Salt Lake City after some deliberation over heading south to Moab. Although Moab would have been a great pitstop, we had an AirBnB booked in Salt Lake and Moab would have put us behind a day. Once agreeing that we should stay on schedule, Maggie admitted the need to relieve herself so we pulled off at an empty roadside rest stop. The air conditioning inside the car kept us cool but the outside looked scorchingly hot.

"Here we are," said Maggie, putting the car in park. "Once I shut this thing off we're probably going to get really freaking hot. You ready?" she asked, hand lingering on the ignition.

"No," I said. "Wait a sec."

Unbuckling my seat belt, I swiftly leaned over and pressed myself against Maggie, immediately swooping in for a kiss. Our lips met and our kiss began. I could tell Maggie was first caught off guard but she soon melted into it. Her hand reached over and gripped onto my shirt, the two of us each beginning to gently groan as our kiss grew heated.

Our mouths opened and tongues came out, lightly mingling, and I started feeling around on her body, looking for something to hold onto. The sun beat in through the windshield but the AC kept us cool. I could feel my breathing grow more labored as I ardently made out with my wonderful and beautiful friend.

Slowly, I pulled back. Maggie and I simultaneously opened our eyes and looked at one another. Smiles grew across our lips. Maggie stifled a small laugh and she appeared both embarrassed and excited. It was a pretty sweet moment, pretty powerful if I'm being straight. Sure, we had already had sex, both that time with Piper and the morning after together in our bedroom, but there was something about this sudden kiss that made me feel so much more intimate with Maggie. I could tell she felt it too.

"What was that for?" she asked softly through her smile.

"I just wanted to do it," I said.

"Are you coming on to me, Dana?" Maggie said teasingly. Bringing her hand up, she put her finger to the corner of her lip.

"I might be," I said.

"You know I really have to pee," she murmured, putting on a sexy tone to humorously contrast with what she was actually saying.

"You always have to pee," I replied in a similar tone.

"Open your mouth," she said. There was a beat of silence until we both broke out into laughter. I smacked her arm lightly. Then, with adoration, Maggie leaned in and pushed a swift kiss to my lips.

It was really hot outside. Over 100 degrees, but very dry. I waited for Maggie outside of one of the rest stop stalls. In the time we had been there, a few other cars had pulled in, travelers like us spilling out into the scenery, walking around the craggy overlook, traipsing up the ascension that offered a small covered bench. It was calming. It was pleasant. Nobody seemed rushed. They just took out their cameras, posed, snapped photos, had a respite from the long drive they were on.

The door to the stall popped open and Maggie came out.

"Ugh," she groaned as she stepped back into the daylight, wiping her wet hands on her shorts. "Unless you really have to go," Maggie said. "Don't go in there."

"Did you wreck it?" I asked with a glimmer in my eye.

"No!" she protested and laughed. "No, that bathroom was already wrecked before I got my turn."

"Was it really that bad?"

"Um, *yes*," she said. "I feel like I need a shower. No toilet paper, no paper towels. I'm thankful there was a sink in there."

"So if I hold your hand it shouldn't be *too* gross?" I asked. "Right?"

"Right," Maggie smiled. She reached her hand out and I took it.

Together we walked up the slope toward a small desert overlook. To either side of us, we could see lizards slinking around, running scared as we approached them. It warmed my heart to hold onto Maggie's hand, though I certainly didn't need to feel any warmer. The heat was oppressive and the sun was bright. If we weren't in shorts and sunglasses, things might not have been so peachy.

"My feet are going to get so dirty," remarked Maggie, looking down to her flip-flops. She absently kicked a small stone out of her way.

"I guess that's just part of our desert vacation," I mused,

yanking her closer to me as we walked hand-in-hand. Maggie purred softly as she nestled into me. I felt her hair against my bare arm.

"I'm really liking this," said Maggie, offering my hand a squeeze as she spoke. I knew what she meant.

"Me too."

"I always kinda had a thing for you, Dana," Maggie said sweetly. It was a revelation to hear that. We had been such close friends for a long time and I had never seen it. Or maybe I just hadn't *wanted* to see it.

"Really?" I said. "I find that hard to believe."

"No, really!" she said with a bright smile, tugging at my hand. "But c'mon, what was I going to do? You were into dudes. I wasn't trying to be some predator!" We laughed together.

"Yeah, I guess I might have been slightly offended," I said. "If not secretly intrigued."

"I mean, you're so super pretty," Maggie said. "And you're fun and funny and sweet. We've always had a good time together."

"That's true."

"What do you think of me?" she said through an innocent grin, turning to look at me as we stopped at the apex of the short climb.

"I think you're surrounded by incredibly beautiful mountains," I smiled.

"Cut it out!" said Maggie, lightly smacking me on the arm. She looked behind herself and saw those enormous ranges, tall and imposing, jaggedly carved into the majestic landscape around us. "I mean, *yes*, it's beautiful… of course! Do you find yourself slowly becoming unimpressed by all this?" she said in mock-seriousness. "When *everything* is amazing, it's like *nothing* is amazing!"

"You're a dork," I said, unable to wipe the happy smile off my face.

"So c'mon," Maggie said, softening, her hand petting my arm now. "What do you think about me?" The tone was suddenly very intimate, almost serious, but still pleasant and warm and accepting. It felt like an important moment.

"Maggie," I said, trying to find the words. "I mean… *yeah*! I've always felt so incredibly close to you. I've always thought you were a great person, an admirable person. And you're gorgeous! Like, *seriously*. Do you really need me to say it?"

"Yes," Maggie said simply. "You don't think I'm a little runt? You know, because I'm so short?" I laughed tenderly at her.

"No way," I said. "I've always adored you. If you had come on to me when we were younger, I mean, I probably wouldn't have done anything about it. But inside… I would have probably been filled with such an intense desire for you. The same as I feel right now."

"That's good to know." Maggie grinned and scrunched her nose up, causing her sunglasses to lift up slightly.

"Look," I said. "I've got to tell you. I'm really confused and torn up. This is tough for me. But I'm also really enjoying this liberation. Out here," I said, spreading my arms out. "I'm just some stranger. Nobody knows me as

Dana Cox. I'm just a random person who can hold hands with you and kiss you and nobody knows my past."

"Cox," repeated Maggie, sticking her tongue out. "Girl, you *need* to change your name back."

"Are you ruining my moment of opening up to you?" I said with a skeptical laugh. But it was expected. This was how Maggie and I always interacted. I loved how playful we were together.

"No, of course not," she said. "But Cox? Like Dana Dicks. Dana Pen—"

"Stop!" I said, holding my hand up. "I promise I'll change my name back soon, despite what a pain in the ass it'll be."

"Your maiden name was so much nicer," mused Maggie with a wistful smile. "Dana Darling. Because you're such a darling."

"Right," I said, rolling my eyes.

"Well, Dana *Darling*," Maggie said, continuing on. "I'm glad whatever this is that's happening between us… I'm glad it's happening. It's really making me happy to have *this* with one of my best friends."

"Me too," I said. I smiled with mounting joy as Maggie and I looked at each other. Then, as though we could read each other's minds, we both leaned in and kissed.

After a wonderful moment of silence, we began walking back down the hill and toward the car. I was ready to be back into the air conditioning and I'm sure Maggie was as well.

"I do have a question for you," I said as we walked.

"What happened between you and Piper that it didn't work out? You know, so I can try to avoid that fate." I grinned.

"Control freak," Maggie grinned back. "She might seem easygoing, but she's a bit crazy. Really hot, *definitely*, but a bit too much for me."

"And it's not going to make anything weird between us?" I asked, gripping onto Maggie's hand tightly. "You know, what we did with her?"

"Oh my God, *no!*" she said. "Are you kidding? Piper is a total fox and I'm glad we got to do that together. Heck, if it hadn't happened, we might not be *here* right now." With that, Maggie held up our knitted hands and smiled at me.

"You might be right," I said. Then, simply, I affirmed it all. "Cool."

It was overwhelming how happy I was. I felt my eyes well up with tears. Maybe I was just getting crazy from the heat. Or maybe this was what real happiness felt like. Either way, I didn't think I'd ever feel like this in life. I didn't know this kind of happiness existed. And I was greedy for more of it.

———

"So this is the place," said the young woman, Mallory was her name, standing there in front of us in tight black yoga pants and a tank top. She had muted auburn hair tumbling down in curated ringlets. Her grin was wide and her teeth were big. "It's not much but it should be a great home base for your stay in Salt Lake City."

"Thanks!" said Maggie brightly, looking around. The entrance to Mallory's condo put you immediately in the kitchen, which then lead out to a small living room with a small couch. There was no television, but there was a flatscreen aluminum computer to the side of the couch. A staircase off the living room lead upwards to a loft, over the kitchen, where the large bed lived. "I like it. It's very calming."

"I'm a yoga teacher," said Mallory matter-of-factly. "Oh! I have mats rolled up over against the far wall," she said, pointing. "The sun comes in through the big window in the morning and it's a great time to practice."

"We'll keep that in mind," I said.

"Also," continued Mallory as we walked through her condo. "I don't know if you knew this, but on Sundays in Salt Lake City you can't buy any alcohol. So I made sure to get you a bottle of wine in case you were looking to relax." She motioned to the coffee table in the living room, upon which sat the wine, two glasses, and a corkscrew.

"That's so super sweet of you," said Maggie. "We would have had no idea about that law."

"Is this your first time doing AirBnB?" asked Mallory.

"We did it on our way out," said Maggie. "In Omaha."

"Very cool," said Mallory. "So I've just got a little instruction list over there in the kitchen with all the specifics. Feel free to text me with any questions. And really, eat anything you want that I have around. The bananas, especially. And if they go bad while you're here, don't feel bad about tossing them. Cool?"

"Cool," Maggie and I said together.

"So are you just friends traveling together or…" said Mallory, looking back and forth between us.

"Yep," said Maggie. "Just traveling together. We're hoping to do some hiking." I could see the smarmy grin on Maggie's lips.

"Oh terrific," said Mallory. "I left some brochures on the coffee table about all the stuff to do around here. You're going to have a blast."

"Definitely," said Maggie.

"So I'm going to take off," Mallory said, wrapping it all up. "I'll be staying with my boyfriend. Like I said, just text with any questions." With that, Mallory handed off the keys to Maggie.

"Thanks," said Maggie. "We're really looking forward to it."

After some more pleasantries, Mallory said goodbye and left us standing in her condo with our bags slumped down on the hardwood floor. Maggie and I were both feeling quite exhausted from driving.

"That wine sounds good," Maggie said absently.

"Yeah," I said. "I'm game."

"I'm going to shower first," she said. "How about you?"

"I should do that, too," I said. "I'm feeling pretty sticky."

"How about you go first," Maggie said with a sweet smile. "I'm going to plop down on that couch and close my eyes for a few."

I smiled and nodded.

Once showered, I posted up on the couch in fresh

lounge shorts and a tank, eagerly opening the wine bottle to pour myself a glass. I just relaxed into the small two seater couch, feet up on the coffee table, looking through a brochure, sipping my wine. I felt tired but the shower had helped revitalize me. Maggie and I didn't really have any plans for the evening, probably just a quick run out to some restaurant for dinner, as our real explorations would begin the following day. Being in a new space, in this young woman Mallory's place, it was a nice feeling. It wasn't like you were in a hotel. It felt lived in and comfortable.

As I meditated on how our time in Salt Lake City might go, inspired by the brochures Mallory had left, I heard the bathroom door crack open and I looked to my left. With a smile on her face, Maggie slinked out, her blonde hair darkened from dampness, a cream colored towel wrapped around her short lissome body.

"You're already drinking without me?" she whined, scurrying up to the coffee table. "Pour me one too!"

"Of course," I said, grinning up at her. Taking hold of the bottle, I slowly poured her glass full and once I had done so, Maggie quickly snatched it up and took a sip.

"You better not already be half way through that bottle," she said. Her face was a beautiful alabaster white, devoid of any makeup. Her eyebrows looked a little thinner, eyes a little less pronounced. But Maggie was stunning, with or without a painted face. My heart beat quickened as I appreciated her prettiness.

"I was good," I smirked.

"Good," she countered firmly, taking another drink.

Holding her towel to her chest with one hand, Maggie leaned down and set her glass back on the coffee table.

"Not a bad shower, eh?" I said.

"Good pressure!" said Maggie. "Did you go exploring the house at all while I was in there?"

"Like riffling through that girl's stuff?" I asked with a short laugh. "No."

"Let's do it!" said Maggie with a light in her eyes. "It'll be fun." Maggie tightened her towel and secured it with a tight fold into itself at her breast and then scurried over to her duffel bag. Picking it up, she motioned for me to follow with her head. Without thinking much more about it, I stood up from the couch and followed Maggie as she ascended the stairs up to the lofted bedroom.

"This bed is nice and big," said Maggie as we reached the loft, tilting her head slightly. "Look at all those wicker baskets underneath. I bet that's her clothes and stuff."

"Maggie," I chastised, following her still as she explored. "We can't go through her stuff. C'mon."

"I'm not going to do anything bad," countered Maggie with a devilish grin. She got down on her hands and knees next to the bed, looking at the baskets and choosing one to take out. As she did this, the towel she wore inched up her backside and exposed her just slightly. I could make out the subtle curve of her pleat, her fur shower damp, and I suddenly felt an aroused excitement move through me.

"She'll know if we go through her stuff," I said, still feeling a bit anxious about Maggie's invasion but secretly enjoying it. I especially enjoyed the view of Maggie down on the floor.

"C'mon," she said, looking back at me with joy in her face. "We're on vacation. It's an adventure."

"You're still in a towel," I said, arms crossed, slightly looking away. But I kept an eye on Maggie's wiggling backside, sneaking a peek at her intimacy.

"I'm feeling frisky," Maggie mused, sliding out the wicker basket nearest the head of the bed and looking into it. "This chick has nice taste in panties." Pulling out a pink lacy thong, Maggie held it up to me and smiled.

"You're impossible!" I said, unable to suppress my laughter. "Put that away."

"Maybe I'll just wear it!" said Maggie, still holding up the underwear, a plaintive look on her face.

"Mags!" I protested. "Get off the floor. I don't know what's gotten into you."

"Oh my," she remarked, ignoring me, still sorting through the basket. "Here's the goods."

"What?" I said, softening, Maggie's tone beginning to pique my interest.

"Behold!" said Maggie, hoisting up her find into the air. It was a dark purple silicone dildo. A nice size. And with curves too. It looked like it had been an expensive purchase.

"No," I said, shaking my head. "Maggie, put that away. We need to stop going through this girl's stuff." Maggie jumped up from the floor, the toy still in her hand, that incorrigible grin plastered across her face.

"It looks like fun," said Maggie in a singsong voice,

slowing edging toward me, wagging the piece in my direction.

"Some other chick's sex toy?" I replied. "We don't know where it's been."

"I know exactly where it's been," countered Maggie. "In that pretty yoga girl's snatch!"

"Ugh!" I groaned, tossing my head back. Maggie laughed at me.

"Think fast!" said Maggie suddenly. Before I knew it, the purple toy was flying toward me and instinctively I reached out and caught it.

"Hey!"

"Nice catch," said Maggie. Then, with a swift pull, Maggie undid her towel and yanked it off her body, dropping it to the ground. Her supple, slim body was revealed to me. My eyes moved over her pert breasts, the gentle curve of her slim belly, down to her enticing mound of blonde damp fur. I took a deep breath as I looked upon her. Maggie had this impishness in her eyes, a sultry naughtiness that I couldn't deny.

"Okay," was all I could say.

"I haven't even asked you to do anything," she grinned. Stepping up closer to me, it wasn't much longer until our lips pressed together and we began a long, luxurious kiss causing me a shortness of breath and the redoubling of my arousal. With the purple toy in one hand, I wrapped my other hand around Maggie and pressed it against the small of her back. I could feel the heat coming from her.

This thing that was happening between Maggie and I

was moving so fast and I was completely engulfed by it. Normally, I wouldn't have been so quick to become intimate with somebody. But then again, my experiences in the past were all with men and I was never too eager for them. With Maggie, our friendship went so far back and my adoration for her was so deeply ingrained. I had never been aware before how much I cared for her. How genuinely I loved her.

"Mmm," moaned Maggie as she slowly pulled her lips back from mine. "Dana," she murmured against my mouth. "You've gotta fuck with me that thing."

"I don't *gotta* do anything," I countered in a mimicked whisper.

"You *better* fuck with me that thing."

I just about lost it right there, my knees feeling weak, my belly feeling queasy. She had me.

Our kissing went on for a few more minutes, the two of us standing there near the bed, Maggie nude against me while I was feeling heated even in my small amount of clothing. I felt myself growing moist between the legs, my body obviously readying itself, and my mind was swimming in Maggie's unabashed sensuality.

Then she pulled back from me and stepped away, pivoting on her heel, and climbing up onto the bed. Like I was under hypnosis, I followed, mounting the bed behind her and watching as Maggie crawled up the blanket. She gently positioned her head into the pillows while remaining up on her knees, rear in the air, presenting her gorgeous underside for my perusal. Slowly, Maggie wiggled her ass back and forth. I couldn't fight it after that — not that I really wanted to — and the switch in my brain had been flipped.

I sat up behind Maggie and tenderly moved my hand between her thighs, pressing it upwards against the downiness of her soft sex, feeling immediately its wetness and suppleness. Moving my hand back and forth against her slit, I couldn't help but stare into her privacy. The gentle hair covering her was pale and light, her rear offered a small pink little folded knot, and the lips of her pussy were full and prone and revealing the pinkness of her inner life with a glistening sheen.

The toy fell out of my hand and onto the bed as I closed in on Maggie's wonderful behind. I placed a hand on her rump to steady myself as I increased the fervor of my petting. I could tell she loved it from the vocal pleasure coming from her mouth.

"Yeah," she oozed, her chest heaving as it took in a long deep breath. Maggie nuzzled harder into the pillows and sheets, butt still slowly wiggling at me but not so much for me to lose my focus. She was getting wetter moment by moment and I saw a few beads of sweat roll from the small of her back up toward her shoulders.

I leaned my face down and placed a soft kiss on one of her cheeks. This made Maggie offer back a deeply contented sigh.

"Here," Maggie said. Then, reaching her arm back, she wrapped her fingers around my wrist and guided my hand. She moved me closer to the split of her rear, letting me loose as my thumb landed between her cheeks. "I like my ass played with."

"Yeah?" I softly whispered with a bit of surprised.

"Mm hmm."

And I obliged. Pressing my thumb gingerly against her knot, I slowly caressed it in a concentric circle while my opposing hand ran back and forth over her heated pinkness. With each pass, I gave her lips a loving squeeze, offering some firm pressure both up front and in back.

"Oh God," Maggie moaned, her hips squirming slightly side to side. "That's nice."

Although I was inexperienced with giving anybody attention to their ass, I have to admit I was transfixed by it. My heart was racing impossibly fast and I couldn't take my eyes off of my own slow movements. I could feel the gentle creases of Maggie's backside, the tiny folds, the subtle gap that would ever slightly open and close with Maggie's increasingly laborious breaths. I was feeling incredibly aroused, like I was buzzing, like my stomach was tying itself in knots. I loved it.

Then, almost as though they had a mind of their own, my middle and ring fingers pressed together and entered Maggie's wet blossom. She groaned loud and clenched her stomach as I began my thrusts. The musky scent of sex wafted up into my nose, inspiring me increase the speed of my steady penetrations. Meanwhile, my thumb pushed against her rear dot, as though it were some amazing button that would increase the volume of her lusty exhales. I was eager to hear her moans.

NICOLETTE DANE

"Mm hmm, "Maggie affirmed. "I like that."

Maggie's underside was flush and glimmering, her lips parting to either side as I pushed my fingers inside of her, her wonderful sex absorbing my digits with the faintest squishing sounds. Staring down at her, admiring her, my heart feeling full, I realized how much I loved doing this. This felt perfect. This felt like what I was supposed to be doing.

"Toy," she groaned out in a breathy exhale. "Mmm!"

"Okay," I said, nodding slowly, looking around to find where I had laid the purple totem. I slowly eased my fingers from Maggie, my fingers coated by her wet love, and reached for the dildo. Hoisting it up, I gazed upon it and a smile crept over my face. Before I had protested it because I'd felt weird about it. But now, in this lust-drunk state, I was excited to please.

I pointed the toy at Maggie's slit and slowly pressed against her lips. Her pussy wantonly accepted the silicone, lips parting, opening up, allowing it to slip into her. And as it entered, pressuring her insides all around, Maggie released a deep moan, almost a gurgle, as her back arched and her head craned up.

"Oh fuck," she said very slowly.

"Oh my God," I mused as I started to pull the dildo out, press it back in, and pull it out again. Maggie's juices coated the toy easily, globules of white creaminess sticking to it each time I retrieved it, a single tacky string of unbroken essence held between Maggie's achy lips and the shaft, elastic and viscid.

118

"That feels just fucking wonderful," Maggie said, her head shaking back and forth. With my patterned thrusting, Maggie's backside and hips mimicked the movements, moving back when I pulled out and forward when I pressed in. Each breath that left her lips was audible, hot and steamy, and I watched as she brought a hand up and readjusted a large bundle of her blonde hair that had gotten into her face.

I was tingling. I felt like I was watching myself in a movie. Like I was on autopilot somehow, just doing whatever naturally came to me in order to please my lover. I wanted to touch her all over. I wanted to feel her sticky flesh against mine, her hot breath against my neck. But most of all, I wanted her to come. That was the most prominent thought in my brain as my wrist flicked and the toy slipped inside of her. I wanted Maggie to scream out in delight.

Remembering her admitted desires from earlier, I once more pressed my thumb against her rear and gave her more sustained pressure this time. Maggie cried out in passion and wriggled. She looked back at me and our eyes met. Frantic with lust, Maggie nodded her head quickly. I could see the humid glistening of sweat on her face. She was desperate for it.

By now the crevice between her legs was moistened from our love, and I started kneaded my thumb against her ass, back and forth, up and down, as she grinded back against me and the impaling purple staff. I could tell she was short of breath. I could tell she was restless and longing for it. God, was she beautiful. As Maggie rode against my motions, quicker now, I saw the backs of her thighs start to quiver. This only made me increase the speed of my wrist and pet her rear even firmer still.

"Mm hmm," Maggie confirmed steadily, head bobbing. "Mm hmm, mm *hmm!*"

I could feel her backside clench, her pussy gripped tightly onto the toy and squeezed, her rear contracted. At first Maggie's hips squirmed slowly in some sort of haphazard figure eight. Then the pace of her movements exponentially quickened, her butt jerking and twisting uncontrollably. She was panting, crying out, whining. Her legs pumped, thighs juddering, under she exploded in a loud gasp and her entire backside fell down to the bed where she spasmed like she was having a seizure. The dildo had slid out of her when she crumpled down, but I just continued holding it in my hand as I watched her shakily journey through orgasmic bliss.

I loved her. I mean, I know that's a sudden revelation. But I'd also felt close to her, always loved her as a close friend, but sharing this intimacy with her made me only want to do it again and again. I wanted these brilliant moments always. I wanted her to want the same for me. I wanted us both to just be happy. That's love in my mind. That's what it's all about. Do whatever you can to make one another happy.

"Oh fuck," cooed Maggie, smacking her hand on the bed. She then slithered that same hand between her legs and tenderly caressed herself. "Dana, I think I put a huge wet spot on this blanket."

"That's okay," I said gently with a smile on my face. I dropped my free hand to her rump and ran it over her pale skin. "I'm still holding the dildo. I don't know why."

"Just set it down," said Maggie through a laugh. Having regained control of her figure post-orgasm, Maggie rolled over onto her back, propping herself up with the pillows, and grinned at me. I assayed her small body, my eyes caught on the matted and moist blonde fur between her thighs.

"Okay," I said, letting the dildo fall down onto the bed.

"And c'mere," said Maggie, beckoning me toward her with a single finger.

I crawled up next to her and the two of us wrapped around each other in a contented embrace. I could feel Maggie's stabilizing breath against me. Absentmindedly, my hand fell down to her mound and delicately played with her damp hair.

"Mmm," she intoned through a smile, her butt grinding down into the sheets. "Thank you."

"That made me really happy," I said. "To give you an orgasm. I was so happy to do it."

"I will accept an orgasm from you, dear, anytime you want to give it," Maggie sung.

"We've got a week here all alone," I said, happiness overtaking me as I spoke. "We don't even have to leave this condo." Maggie giggled.

"That is a really wonderful idea," she said. "Though I would feel bad coming all this way and not exploring the city."

"I guess we could do both," I teased.

Maggie hummed a little noise of delight. Then, after a few beats, she spoke up again.

"Dana," she said. "You're the best." I felt her arms wrap tighter around me.

"You are," I countered. "I can't believe I'm doing this," I said. "Any of this."

"I can't believe things are working out like this," said Maggie. "But I don't want any of it to end." I felt her kiss the side of my head and nuzzle her nose against my hair.

"Me neither," I agreed. "This is… *wonderful.*"

"Did you hear that?" said Maggie suspiciously, looking around through the trees and brush alongside the thin worn trail underneath our shoes. "Was *that* a rattlesnake?"

"Maybe," I said, looking side to side to see if I could spot it. The trail we were on, called Diamond Fork, was nestled into the desert mountains of Utah about an hour outside of Salt Lake City. According to Maggie's pre-trip research, the hot springs at the end of this trail were not to be missed. But the stick in her spokes was that Maggie was not too fond of snakes and Diamond Fork was known for its rattlers.

"My heart's racing," she said. "That couple who passed us said they saw one."

"If we do see one," I said. "We just need to stay out of its way and let it slither by."

"If we see one, I'm probably just going to run the other way," said Maggie with nervous laughter.

"C'mon," I said, lifting my brow and smiling at her. I took Maggie by the arm and hurried her along.

There were some treacherous spots on the path, spots in which we had to walk single file just to get across, else we might slide down into the river below to the right of us. Although we were indeed in a desert climate, the trail was lined with trees sticking out of the browned earth. I admired Maggie's cuteness for our hike. She was dressed in patterned blue running shorts, pretty short I might add, a white tank, and a worn pair of running shoes. But the cutest thing of all was that she had knitted her hair into two big chunky braids hanging from the back of her head and over her shoulders. Both of us had swimsuits on under our hiking clothes as we were intent on jumping into the hot springs and messing around.

"Wouldn't it be cool if there was this kind of nature back in Chicago?" asked Maggie, watching each step she took in case she stumbled upon a snake. I could tell she was nervous.

"Well, there's Starved Rock," I said. "That's a nice hike."

"It is," Maggie affirmed. "But *c'mon*." She motioned to the tranquil mountain beauty surrounding us. Steep craggy slopes surrounded us, a gurgling river ran to our side, the landscape off in the distance was dotted with firs.

"Yeah," I replied. "It's nothing like this."

"Maybe we should move out here!" Maggie beamed.

"Move to Boulder or something. I'm still feeling enchanted by that place."

"It just seems so expensive," I countered. "Even more so than Chicago."

"Yeah," said Maggie in agreement. "It's just so pretty out in this part of the country."

"Stop," I said suddenly, taking one more step in from of Maggie and sticking my arm out to block her.

"What?"

"Don't move," I said.

About ten feet ahead of us a very large snake in desert brown with darker brown diamonds on its back began to slither across the path. I took a deep breath and watched. I could feel Maggie shake through my arm as I continued to block her. Her hand slipped around my waist and held onto me. Even through the sound of the river, we could hear the telltale clamor of the creature's imposing rattle.

"That snake," said Maggie slowly. "Is fucking huge."

"Um, yeah," I said. "That's a big snake."

"I think I just peed a little bit," said Maggie. I couldn't help but laugh. "You think that's funny?"

"I do," I said, still snickering. "You didn't pee."

"Just a little!" she protested, reaching down and feeling herself through her shorts. "I'm just glad I'm in a swimsuit."

"Stop it," I said, trying to stifle my smile, shaking my head. "Look, he's almost gone." The snake had just about finished crossing our path, making it's way through the brush toward the steep descent that lead down to the river.

"Thank God," said Maggie. "Let's just wait a little longer and let him do his thing."

As we waited, we lovingly held on to one another. And after a moment, we both looked at each other and smiled.

"Let's get moving," I said.

There weren't many other people on the trail, one of the benefits to coming on this hike at Diamond Fork during the week. We did see other hikers sporadically, though, and at one point an entire troupe of kids walked by us in the opposite direction. It was as though they were on some sort of class trip, though school must have been out for the summer already. Maybe it was a summer camp thing.

"I'm glad we missed all them," said Maggie dramatically. "Can you imagine what the hot springs would be like with all those kids splashing around?"

"Right," I said. "And how would we ever go nude in the springs?"

"Ha!" Maggie belted out. "Are you going to go in naked?"

"I don't know," I said with a hint of embarrassment. "I've thought about it. The brochure said people do it and to not be surprised if you come upon naked people. Why not me?"

"I'd just worry that one of those snakes might slither in," said Maggie, suddenly holding herself and shivering. "I don't want one of those things to crawl up my lady parts."

"I highly doubt that's going to happen," I said, placing a hand on her bare shoulders. I could feel the sweat on her.

"I'd be more afraid of a bunch of teenagers stumbling upon us and gawking."

"Yeah," said Maggie through a laugh. "Can't have that."

"You know they'd be staring at you," I said with a loving smile. "You're a stone cold fox."

"Aw, *c'mon*," she said, bumping her hip into mine. "You're embarrassing me."

"Give me your hand," I said. Taking Maggie's hand, we continued our hike, once again smiling as we looked into one another's glowing faces.

Traversing our way over the rough terrain, avoiding ankle-rolling rocks and swatting at annoying bugs that flew in our faces, Maggie and I eventually made it to the springs. Although we were wearing sunglasses, I knew we both had wide eyes as we stared on at the beautiful waterfall that ran down into a handful of pools. A family of four played around underneath the waterfall while a smattering of other hikers hovered around the springs, some hesitant to get in, while others jumped in without a care in the world. As the path we were walking moved closer to the river, Maggie and I decided to remove our shoes and socks so that they wouldn't get wet. Cautiously, we stepped over the increasingly rocky and wet ground to approach the natural cascade.

"I thought there were more pools than this," mused Maggie as we closed in. "How could you go naked here? It's so public!"

"I don't know," I shrugged.

"Super pretty, though," she said.

"Definitely," I said. "Wanna go in?"

Maggie nodded swiftly and grinned.

The two of us quickly stripped down to our bikinis, tossing our hiking clothes and shoes into a pile off to the side of the river. Maggie broke away first and eagerly made her way toward the waterfall, sometimes scurrying, sometimes carefully stepping on a particularly precarious rock. She wore a navy and white striped bikini, matching bottom and top, and I loved watching her move. Her bottoms allowed you to catch a nice glimpse of her round bum.

I followed her but couldn't catch up with her in time for Maggie to plunge into the waterfall, her entire body becoming immediately drenched. She squealed as the water hit her, laughing maniacally, waving her arms frantically.

"Oh my *God*!" she cried out as I neared her, her voice muffled by the roaring sound of the falls. "It's so freakin' cold!"

"Maybe I *don't* want to get in…"

"Get in here!" commanded Maggie. Reaching out, Maggie took my arm in both her hands and yanked me into the water. As soon as the water hit me, I yelped out. It was much colder than I was expecting but it actually felt pretty good in the desert heat we'd just spent the last hour or so walking through. The water coursed over my hair, matting it down against my body, and I felt completely drenched after only being under for a couple of seconds. The roar of the waterfall was almost deafening.

Maggie leapt out of the falls and I speedily followed her. Both of us stood there shivering, laughing, smiling, suddenly loving the Utah heat that had only made us sweat before.

"Holy crap, that's awesome!" said Maggie.

"Your bottoms are falling off," I remarked, grabbing at the back of Maggie's swim bottoms and hitching them up to cover her exposed crack.

"Yeah?" she said laughing, twisting around to look at her backside. "That water hit me pretty hard."

"That's for my eyes only," I said sweetly.

"Ooh la la," teased Maggie, wagging her firm butt in my direction.

Back off to the side of the river, the both of us dripping wet, we collected our clothing into our arms and looked up to the top of the waterfall through streaking sunglasses. The sun beat down on us and it felt great.

"What do you think is up there?" I asked, pointing to the top of the waterfall.

"I don't know," said Maggie. "I don't even see how you get up there."

"There are some people coming down the side of the hill," I said. "They must have gotten up there somehow."

Still in bare feet, Maggie and I started our walk around the side of the waterfall, eventually discovering a lesser worn path. It was steep — very steep — the kind of path on which you sometimes had to get down onto your knees in order to keep your balance in climbing up. I was behind her in our walk and I couldn't stop myself from staring at her butt. I wanted to just reach out and grab it.

Eventually we reached the top of the incline, seeing the origin of the waterfall, our mouths dropping open. We looked at each and grinned wide. There were more hot spring pools up here and the entire area was empty. Looking down to the bottom of the waterfall, we saw all the other people, the families, the couples, splashing around, yelling out, having fun. Up here it was far more tranquil and serene. I couldn't believe it.

"Insane," said Maggie. "Look at this!"

We hurried across the stream, yet careful not to slip, and made our way toward the pools still with clothes under our arms. As soon as we reached the other side, we tossed our clothing into a pile on a dry rock and stepped up to the pool.

The water was bubbling, actual steam coming off the top. It must have been 100 degrees out and that pool would be even hotter. I was feeling giddy by the whole thing. It was just so perfect, so exciting. Maggie slid in first, mouth dropping as she felt the heat. She cried out and shifted her arms back and forth as she grew accustomed to the warmth. I sat down on the flat rock edge, dipping my legs into the pool up to my knees and immediately felt how hot it truly was. At first it was just too hot, but I didn't waver and I soon succumbed to it. I sighed happily.

"You need to get in here totally," said Maggie, sinking down into the hot spring so that her chest buoyed upon slightly, cleavage apparent at the top of the water.

"Is any one watching?" I asked, looking around to all sides, trying to spot if there was anybody else in the vicinity.

"I think it's just us up here."

"Cool," I said, still looking. Once I was appeased that we were indeed alone, I reached behind my back and deftly untied my bikini top, letting it slide down my arms, tossing it off to the side of the pool. I looked down at Maggie, grinned, and scrunched my shoulders in to better display my breasts.

"You mad woman!" said Maggie.

"I figure, we'll probably never be back here," I said, now sliding down into the pool alongside Maggie. I sighed as I eased in to the heat.

"Okay," Maggie said conspiratorially, head tilting, looking around. Once she was satisfied, she too undid her bikini top and pulled it off, exposing her firm and ample chest. As she looked over to me for approval, I grinned deeply and lifted my hand up from under the water, holding up my bikini bottoms.

"Your move," I said.

"*C'mon!*" she called. "I told you I don't want a snake to get up in there." I laughed happily. I was loving our playful back and forth.

"You don't have to," I said, tossing my bottoms outside of the pool and landing them near my top. As I turned back around to address Maggie, I saw her pulling at her own bottoms underneath the water until she finally got them off her feet and held them up above water.

"Happy?" she said. Her tone was annoyed but it was so obviously put on. Maggie was loving it. We both were.

Cuddling up next to each other, we contentedly bathed naked in that bubbling hot spring, the sun beating down, though thankfully the hot spring we were in had some tree cover. You'd think all that heat would be entirely too oppressive, but it was instead quite relaxing and comfortable. It was an amazing scene around us. The top of the waterfall spilling over, a lush forest behind us, the river coursing down next to us. Nobody else in sight. Our own private little natural hot tub.

"This is nice," cooed Maggie as she nestled into me, my arm around her shoulders, thighs touching. "I can't believe we've got this place all to ourselves."

"Maybe we should take advantage of that," I murmured. Maggie smiled and then turned, bringing herself around front of me and pressing against me. Our lips met slowly, sensually, and as she pressed into me and into our kiss, my hands dropped underwater and cradled Maggie's rear. My heartbeat was on the upswing as I melted into this wonderful and hot meditation of lust.

I felt Maggie slip a hand between my thighs and begin stroking me. I groaned into her mouth.

The arousal redoubled inside of me and I ached for her. My kissing grew more fervent, more needy, and my hands explored her backside and pulled Maggie's body tighter up against my own. I felt like I was whining, I wanted her so badly. And being alone with her in that pool, in public no less, it made the entire thing more real, more risky, more rejuvenating.

Interrupting our kiss, I heard I quick squealing scream in the distance and I opened my eyes. I looked past Maggie, who had turned her head to see where the scream had come from, and together we saw a family of four, a husband and wife and two kids, off in the distance near the sloped path we had taken to get up to this vantage. The wife was looking at us, then looking away, then back again, hand over her mouth, as the husband had turned the two children around and was ushering them back down.

"Okay, turn around," said the man.

The kids were protesting but they followed his instructions. While he wasn't looking in our direction as he began his descent, the wife was still peeking over at us as she went along with her family. I actually thought she was kind of cute.

With hearts racing, Maggie and I were gripping tight to one another. We looked deeply into one another's eyes, each of us with a silly and excited grin across our lips. It was so thrilling to have been seen, to have been caught, and I knew we both felt it. It sent my arousal through the roof and before I knew it, the two of us had returned to furiously kissing, touching, caressing, bathing there in that steamy spring.

It was definitely one of the most randomly sexy and thrilling moments of my life. I never wanted it to end.

Later on, when Maggie and I had left the pool, we were dressed once more in our clothes and hiking back to the car. Hair wet but drying in the sun. I wasn't exactly sure how she felt, but I knew I was incredibly amped up and aroused. The heavy petting hadn't resulted in any orgasms but I knew those would come. I knew there would be so much time for that. And it was almost all I could think about. I wanted to roll around with Maggie in bed, I wanted to touch her and feel her and fuck her. In that moment, I felt far more like a sexual being than I'd ever felt before.

"Hey Maggie," I said, breaking the silence of our hike but not breaking our stride.

"Yeah?"

"I'm really... just, like... falling for you," I admitted, feeling a great sense of relief after saying it.

Maggie looked back at me and offered just the sweetest, most encouraging smile I'd ever seen on her face. It was otherworldly in its joy. It was reassuring and loving and accepting. It made the world feel whole.

"I've already fallen for you," she said. After a moment, Maggie's eyes returned to the trail and we resumed our walk. I was floating.

A few days later we spent the late morning and afternoon cruising around downtown Salt Lake City. We explored Temple Square and the Mormon church site, we hit Red Butte Gardens and walked through that wonderful botanical dream, and ended our day at a highly lauded sushi restaurant in the heart of the city. I was a little trepidatious about eating sushi midweek in the middle of the desert, but it was surprisingly some of the best sushi I'd ever had. And that's coming from someone who's a bit of a sushi connoisseur back in Chicago.

Maggie and I agreed that we were finding Salt Lake City to be just a bit strange. Nothing *bad*, mind you, just kind of an odd place. Maybe you've noticed it if you've visited. Or maybe you're oblivious to it if you live there.

"It's the high altitude," Maggie said with a laugh. "Not enough oxygen around here for people to operate properly. I know I feel a bit loopy!"

We both had a laugh at that. Regardless, I couldn't quite pinpoint it. Everybody we met was incredibly nice. There was just a weird feeling we got from the city as a whole.

"You know what I find odd?" I said to Maggie as we were coming up to our AirBnb. The building was setup almost like a motel, where the doors to each of the apartments were actually outside. We were on the second floor. "The streets are so *wide* here, but there are so few cars on the road."

"*Right?*" affirmed Maggie. "Super wide avenues, like six lanes wide, but no cars."

"It's not an incredibly populous city," I measured. "But it's not like it's totally dead or anything."

"Oh, *wait!*" she said as though a lightbulb had brightened above her head. "I read about this. I remember now. The streets are so wide so that the horse-drawn carriages — you know, *before* cars obviously — so that they could do a turnaround in the street."

"Interesting," I said, pushing the key into the doorknob and then opening up our air conditioned sanctuary.

"Ah!" Maggie sighed, pushing past me and scurrying into the cool air. "That's what mama needed." As she shimmied inside, her rear bounced back and forth, her baby blue cotton skirt sashaying as her hips swayed, arms akimbo.

"This place is an excellent home base," I remarked,

looking around, tossing the keys on the kitchen counter. "It's been really comfortable."

"We'll leave her a good review," grinned Maggie, face scrunching up and giving me a wink.

"Hopefully she'll leave us a good review, too," I replied, wagging my finger at Maggie. She cackled.

Up in the lofted bedroom was a door that lead out to a deck and Maggie and I grabbed a wine bottle, some glasses, a corkscrew, and headed out there. The sun was beginning to set off to the west, and our view was magical. Those beautiful southwest oranges and yellows and browns colored the mountain range that surrounded Salt Lake City. Sure, it was warm out there there on the deck but it was worth it to see another Utah sunset.

"I can't believe we're almost done with Salt Lake already," mused Maggie, sipping her wine, sighing, gazing out into the sky. "This trip feels like it's going so quickly."

"Wouldn't it be cool to keep driving west?" I said. "Out to California."

"That would be *so* cool," she said. "But *ugh*," Maggie said with a dissatisfied groan. "Once I get back home I've got to put together some lesson plans and coordinate my classes with the registrar's office."

"Yeah," I hummed. "I don't have much more time off work either. Just enough for our drive back to Chicago."

"What a pisser," said Maggie. Her disgust quickly turned to happiness. Lifting her glass toward me, she continued on. "But I'm so pumped that *this* happened."

"Me too," I smiled, almost embarrassingly demure. We clinked our glasses and then both took a sip.

"What's gonna happen when we get back?" said Maggie, looking overtop her browline framed glasses at me as though it were totally up to me to decide.

"What ever do you mean?" I asked in a tease, playing dumb.

"I'm just *saying*," said Maggie, making sort of a goofy voice, like she was screwing around. "When we get back to Chicago are you going to *fuck* me there like you're *fucking* me out here?" The two of us laughed together.

"I mean, what can I say?" I said. "*Yes*, of course. I love this. Maggie, this is just… oh man, this is tremendously liberating. I feel… so, *so* free."

"That's just awesome," she smiled. We both sipped our wine as we looked each other in the eye.

Maggie then stepped closer to me, craned her neck upwards just so, and pressed her wine-moistened lips to mine. We each held our glasses outwards as we kissed, eyes closing, lip locked and in love, hearts racing, a divine calm washing over us. You know, it's funny. I'd heard people say before that their lover was their best friend and I never felt like that with any of the men I'd dated, not even with Paul who I had married. But Maggie truly was my best friend, such a wonderful woman to play around with, and now, with these spectacular new developments, I was finally beginning to experience what it meant to share that kind of bond with your lover.

"Mmm," I sighed as our lips parted. We both smiled and

immediately went for our glasses, sipping, and then giggling. I felt so bemused around Maggie, almost ditzy. That was kind of uncharacteristic of me but I reveled in it. When you feel good, you can't deny it. You embrace it.

"Do you want to go inside?" Maggie asked tenderly.

"OH GOD," I let stumble out of my mouth in a long, low slur like I was over intoxicated. Naked and presenting, I was propped up on my knees with my arms and head buried into the pillows, feeling just extraordinary and tingly, as Maggie pressed her face against me from behind and slowly ate me out. I could feel every subtle movement of her tongue as it ran over my slit, starting from my achy little bead, and coursing back to the base of my pussy. I felt so moist, so impossibly wet that I was probably dripping. Or I would have been dripping had Maggie not lapped it up first.

Maggie then firmly pressed her lips to mine, kissed, sucked, buzzed. My head felt like it was spinning as my hips gyrated and I moaned into the pillows.

With one hand on my rump, Maggie drew her tongue slowly up, licking at my pinkness, up through my crevice, and then I felt the tip of her tongue touch my ass. I'd never felt anything like it before. I had no idea how sensitive I was back there and how unique of a feeling it was. And Maggie wasn't afraid. She dove right in, tracing her tongue around my rim, quickly licking it, before returning downwards once again and kissing my soaked bloom.

"I liked that," I whispered.

"Oh yeah?" I heard come from behind me between licks.

"Mm hmm."

"Good to know." Maggie's finger then pressed against my ass, rubbing in a tender circle, as she continued to kiss my lips. I felt immaculate and I exhaled a pleasured moan into the pillow.

Without missing a beat, Maggie popped up behind me, one hand running up and down my back, the other plunging against my sex. I felt two fingers slip into my wetness, while Maggie's thumb touched my rear, massaging me back there as her wrist began pumping, fingers thrusting. As she leaned down against me, kissing my back, I felt her breasts touch my skin.

"How's that?" Maggie whispered and then kissed again. Her thumb gave an even more pressured push against my bum.

"Good," I said, nodding methodically. "Real good."

"I really love anal stuff," she continued on in a low voice, like she was telling me a well-kept secret. "I don't know why. It just really turns me on."

"Oh yeah?" I said in a pleasured sigh. Her dirty talk was really working on me and I arched my back as I felt her fingers push into me, her thumb continuing to caress.

"Yeah," affirmed Maggie. "Some people think it's weird. But I think *those people* are weird." She giggled happily and pressed harder against my ass. At that moment, I felt my rim dilate just slightly, her thumb tip coaxing me open.

"Yeah," I repeated, as though I were talking to her and not just simply moaning in enjoyment. "*Mmm*, yeah."

"Do you trust me?"

"Mm hmm," I hummed, nodding, fingers gripping into the sheets.

"Okay." I could hear the smile on Maggie's face.

I felt Maggie's hand leave me and she sat up. While she indeed kept her palm resting on one of my cheeks, I felt trapped in anticipation for what might come next. Without her hot breath and wet licks between my thighs, I could feel a slight chill run over my sex. It was a nice respite but I was eager for more attention. I even caught myself reflexively whimpering as I waited.

Then it felt like a bucket of loopy endorphins had been dumped all over my head. Some sort of levy broke, a fulfilling sense of desire washing over me. Maggie had unceremoniously pushed that purple toy we'd uncovered deep into me. She didn't slowly ease it in, she didn't wait for me to accept it, she just pushed firmly and in it went. I was drooling. It was incredible.

"Oh my fucking God," I moaned. "Oh shit."

"You're so wet, Dana," Maggie mused as she penetrating me with a steady flick of her wrist. I felt her finger rub against my pussy, caressing into the wetness, and drawing that moisture upwards toward my crack.

"Oh, that thing feels so good," I called, shaking my head, joy overtaking me. "Keep going."

"Can do," said Maggie sweetly.

The toy easily parted my lips and coursed inside of me,

back and forth, measured and methodical, asserting just an awesome pressure against my cleft. My entire backside was feeling sparkly and magical, everything abuzz with aroused and satisfying awareness. But a certain lapse in my overall awareness left me open for surprise. Suddenly, without knowing what was happening, I felt my backside dilate and Maggie's finger gingerly entered.

"Fuck," I said, pounding my hand on the bed. I clenched, feeling my rim tighten around Maggie's finger. Then she started slowly moving that hand back and forth. Nothing forceful, just an indolent in and out in synch with that silicone staff that was penetrating my womanhood.

It was an experience I wouldn't soon forget. Maggie was probing both my pussy and my ass and I felt just fucking fine.

It was my first time doing such a thing and it made me regretful that I hadn't tried it before. I'd spent 35 years not knowing how much pleasure my body could take. But in that moment, as Maggie attended to my amusement, obviously also amusing herself in the process, I stepped through a new door and I kept walking.

I knew I was whining and groaning, my knees grinding down into the bed, my belly clenching, each thrust from behind pushing me closer to the brink of beatitude. I would have most certainly been embarrassed to be in such a position with any of my past lovers. But with Maggie, she could do anything she wanted to me. I was completely willing to be her pincushion.

"You're so gorgeous," cooed Maggie. "So, so pretty."

"Fuck me," was all I could muster. In the heat of the moment, your mind and body go on autopilot. You get selfish. You just want to be loved hard and fast and without an intermission until you're simply pummeled into submission, lying in a crumpled heap on the bed, shivering and shaking and gasping for air. Whoever or whatever, God or nature, designed sex for women did an amazing job. If you do it right, it's not just a minute or so of grunting and thrusting. It can be a sustained and steady composition of complex and prurient thrill. You just need to open yourself up to feel it. You've got to let it happen.

I was getting so close. I could feel it all bubbling up inside of me. I was reaching for it. I was ready. My breaths were fast and vocal, my knuckles were white as I tore into the sheets. Ass up. Maggie behind me pushing.

Then confusion rushed over me as I felt the toy slip out. While Maggie's finger remained in my rear, my sex was desperately missing the love it had been receiving. My hips were automatically grinding back and forth, as though they were searching for that tool.

"Mm," I groaned. "Mm. Mm." I was whining again. I wanted it so bad.

"Shh," I heard come from Maggie. Her finger slowly eased out of my backside and I quickly felt like I was missing out. I felt empty. But soon enough, Maggie's hand petted through my sopping mound and guided my own juices upward, coating my rear in it, sloppily messing it all around, slimy and sticky and hot.

"Oh fuck, Maggie," I said, my body shivering. "I'm so close. I'm so close."

"I know," she whispered. "Shh."

My stomach dropped when I felt it. With an even compression, Maggie had positioned the dildo against my rear and was coaxing me open. I couldn't believe it. I couldn't believe I was living in that moment. It was new and exciting and different and I didn't want it to stop. I wanted to bottle that novelty and messily drink it. I was so relaxed and eager that it didn't take much at all for my rim to expand and the toy to make it's way inside of my ass. My arms were shaking as I tried to hold myself up. I whimpered and shook as Maggie penetrated me.

"How does that feel?" she asked gently. The piece had disappeared inside of me and then Maggie began the long, slow pull out, only to press it back in again. "Does it feel wet enough?"

"Mm hmm," I whined frantically. I didn't want to talk. I just wanted to be dominated.

"No pain?"

"No," I pleaded. I was so ready to come, so ready to explode. I wanted it. I needed it.

"Good."

Then the thrusts began. Maggie's movements were steady and deliberate. Slipping her other hand between my legs, she adoringly fondled my sore lips, drawing her fingers through my slit, caressing my inner pinkness, using her fingertips to diddle my little sticky pebble. I'd never been fucked so well in my life. I was hypnotized by Maggie's assertions. If she had asked me in that moment to do absolutely anything, I would have agreed. I would have killed for her. I would have been her slave. I would have joined her cult and prayed to her all day and all night. It was just that spectacular.

Inwardly, well, you know how I was feeling. Outwardly, I was drenched in sweat, I was gyrating, I was emitting a constant humming moan. It was like I no longer had control over my body. Maggie had control. She was manipulating me like a puppet. It was a welcome loss of control.

I could feel my body clench and release, trying to hold onto the toy as it entered and exited me. My clutching was reflexive, almost robotic contractions like my rear wanted that toy deeper and deeper inside. There was a mounting numbness moving through me, my fingers and toes, my thighs quivering. Maggie squeezed onto my pussy lips and offered a few firm tugs and it was magic. I moaned and squirmed, my hips bucking. Physically, I could go nowhere. It was my mind that was on a trip.

"Oh God," I cried, feeling my eyes water. "*Mmph!*" My hands slithered up into the pillows and searched for something to hold tight to. My body was shaking. I felt a rawness in my nerves, a tickling, like they were all standing at attention and so ready to be knocked over.

Maggie pressed her palm to my pleat and I could feel the tacky warmth. As she pulled it away, I just knew — *I could feel* — a humid creaminess between my pussy and her hand. It was like I had this heightened sense of awareness. Everything felt specific and nebulous at the same time.

"Oh God," I said again, my backside pumping. "Oh God, oh God…"

Suddenly my body began jerking uncontrollably. Like just flopping around, limbs flailing. I could no longer sit up on my knees and I just collapsed down into the bed. Although I no longer felt Maggie's hand guiding the toy in my bum, the toy was most certainly still there, burrowed inside. I could feel my rim clenching hard to it, my butt bouncing, hips reflexively thrusting down into the bed. I was impossibly sweaty, feeling it on my brow, my neck, my back. As I writhed there into the sheets, it was almost as though I was trying to climb up the bed. Knees moving up and down, arms back and forth.

"Let it take over," I heard Maggie say behind me, her palm kindly rubbing my rump.

And I did. It was like a higher level of orgasm. It just wouldn't stop. And every time my ass clung to the dildo, a brand new electric shiver began its wave through me. I was sobbing like a crazy person, but it was a joyful clamor. Turning to my side now, my hand plunged between my legs and I furiously began petting my throbbing middle. Slowly, steadily, the toy in my rear inched itself out until it flopped down onto the bed behind me. I felt wide open. As I focused on my breathing, my backside opened and closed and opened and closed until it calmly started to return to its tightened form.

"Holy fuck," I said, opening my eyes and looking up at Maggie. She was smiling down at me adoringly.

"Not too bad, huh?"

"I feel like a rag doll," I admitted. "Floppy and loose."

"Yeah, it's pretty good." Maggie grinned knowingly.

"Why have I not tried that before?" I mused, still touching myself. I was returning to full consciousness but every so often I'd experience a sporadic shiver or shake.

"Oh, probably because you thought it would be weird or something," said Maggie, stroking my leg reassuringly. "But I figure, you only get one go at this life. Why not get weird with it?" With that, Maggie giggled.

"Yeah," I agreed, laughing along with her.

"I'm going to get some water," she said with a smile. "You want some?"

"Please."

"Don't move a muscle," she said, giving me a light smack on my thigh where she'd been rubbing. Maggie leapt up from the bed, her small naked body stretched out. She blew a kiss at me and turned, making her way to the loft stairs. I watched as her cute little bum swayed. Then I could only see the limber curve of her back and up. Then just her blonde locks. And then I could only hear her footsteps.

I sighed happily and rolled over onto my back. Underneath my butt was a damp spot on the blanket. But I didn't care. I smiled wide and brought a hand to my chest, leveling my breaths, relaxing, dissolving, unwinding. As I lay there in that supine repose, I was absolutely suffused in love. I felt unchained, unburdened, free. The shackles had been cast off and I was entering a brand new light. This was where Dana Darling belonged.

———

THE NEXT MORNING I woke up with a smile on face, watching as Maggie groggily crawled out of bed, stood up and stretched, slowly walking around the room with her hands on her hips, stretching out her back. I felt my heart melt as I gazed upon her. I knew what was coming. Immediately upon waking up, Maggie would have to run to the bathroom to pee. It was a constant and something I had grown to expect.

She caught me looking at her and she smiled, pushing a blonde tress out of her eyes and tucking it behind her ear. I was so enamored with her. Her lovely nude body before me, lissome and supple, her breasts full and inviting with perfectly round nipples punctuating each of them. And I loved the way her blonde fur covered her down below. Manicured and sculpted, the grain of the hair curving in and pointing directly at her cleft. I'd never found another person more lovely in all my life.

"Morning," she intoned sweetly.

"Morning," I said.

"I have to go pee," said Maggie. "I'll be back."

"I know." I couldn't stop smiling at her.

After an endearingly short wave, Maggie turned and bounced down the stairs. Just as I'd seen her do the night before. Oh, the night before. I could still feel it in my soul. I wanted to feel like that for the rest of eternity.

Once she was gone, I missed her terribly. But I relaxed into the fact that I would soon see her climb those stairs once more, bobbing back and forth, breasts bouncing, and she'd jump back into bed and we'd cuddle and kiss and everything would be right with the world.

But as played this future moment out in my head, my phone began to vibrate on the bedside table. Rolling over once, I took hold of it, unplugged the white cord charger, and looked into it. It was my mother calling.

"Mom?" I said into the phone. She knew I was on vacation. It was very strange for her to be calling me so early.

"Dana," she said. I could tell something was wrong. "Dana... Granny died."

My grandmother. She had been hanging on but barely, wasting away in Hospice care. It's sad that that's how it happens for so many. It's sad that that's how peoples' lives end. But it made me feel powerless. It made me feel like just throwing up my hands. If I could afford my grandmother the best care possible, if I could throw money at the problem to attempt to make it better, I would. But I couldn't. I visited her whenever I was back in my hometown, which was only a couple times a year. I tried to talk to her, but she barely remembered me. God damn it, I was crying.

"Mom," I said through some tears. I brought a finger up and wiped my eye. "Are you okay?"

"It's difficult to lose your mother," she said. I could tell that she was also crying. "We knew this was coming. We're prepared. But you're never completely prepared for something like this."

"When is the funeral?" I asked meekly.

"It will be in two days," she said. "Where are you now?"

"I'm in Utah," I said. "Salt Lake City."

"Well," my mother said with a sigh. "Please don't feel like you need to rush home to attend. I don't want you and your friend to drive crazy or anything. Granny will be cremated and we're just going to have a small service. It's fine."

"Okay," I said, slowly nodding. "Are you sure?"

"I'm sure," she said.

Although on one hand I felt obligated to attend my grandmother's funeral, no matter how small it might be, I also felt this weird sense of relief wash over me. It had been her opinions that had held me back for so long. And even though she had basically been living an incapacitated life for the last year or so, now that she was gone I felt like a weight had been lifted. Maybe that's messed up to say. But life is messed up. That's just how it happens sometimes.

As my mother and I spoke about more specifics, I saw Maggie bound up the stairs just as I'd imagined her to do. Hair swaying, tits hopping, a spring in her step. She was smiling but as soon as she saw me on the phone, a sour face, tears in my eyes, her visage changed to one of concern and she rushed over to my side. I offered a weak smile back to her and reached out for her hand. We threaded fingers and squeezed.

"Thanks Mom," I said. "Send everyone my regards. I wish I could be there. I know I should be there."

"I love you, dear," said my mother.

"I love you, too."

"Text me once you're back in Chicago."

"I will."

"Goodbye, Dana."

"Goodbye, Mom."

I hung up the phone with a long sigh and replaced it on the nightstand. I looked up at Maggie who had a pleading look in her eye.

"Dana…" she mewed. "Is everything okay?"

"My grandmother died," I said, issuing a sustained exhale.

"I'm so sorry," Maggie said through a grimace. She crawled back in to bed next to me and wrapped her arms around me. I gripped tightly to her and absorbed her into a much needed embrace.

"It's okay."

"Do we need to go?" she said softly. "Do we need to drive back this instant?"

"No," I said. "We'll never make it back in time and my mother doesn't want us to rush."

"Okay," said Maggie. She was determined to simply be agreeable and give me whatever I needed. Maggie leaned her neck down and kissed me on the shoulder.

"I mean, I knew this day was coming," I said. "It's a weird feeling. It was expected but, you know, it hits you…"

"I know," said Maggie. "All of my grandparents are gone."

"This was my last one," I said. "It's surreal."

"Very surreal," she said. Then, after a beat. "Don't feel embarrassed to cry if you want."

"Thank you," I said, a fresh tear haphazardly streaking down my cheek.

"I love you, Dana," said Maggie. "I really do."

"I love you, too," I said, holding tighter to her. We hugged so close in that moment it was almost as if we were becoming one. I could think of no better place I could be to absorb this news. A comfortable air conditioned condo rental in Salt Lake City, naked and pressed up against my new beautiful lover, nothing on our agenda but to just be here now. I might have lost it otherwise. But no, even though I was silently crying in Maggie's arms, I had never felt so grateful in all my life. And that was truly comforting.

THREE

"So we just leave the keys on the counter?" I said, hefting my bag up onto my shoulder and looking at Maggie who was staring down into the instructions that Mallory had left for us.

"That's what it says," Maggie replied. "We can lock the door from the inside and just shut it and go."

"Cool," I said, tossing the condo keys to the counter.

"Are you sure you don't want to try to race home?" asked Maggie flatly, giving me a pained yet empathetic look.

"It's okay," I said evenly. "Let's just continue on and try to have fun."

"Okay," she said, letting a smile creep over her face.

We shut the door behind us and on Salt Lake City. Although we both agreed we'd love to continue on west, there was no way we were going to be able to fit it in with the time we had off from work. Thus began our drive back east. We took I-80 up into Wyoming and then jutted up to I-

90. I complained that I wanted to see Yellowstone and Maggie did, too, but that would have to be reserved for another trip. We knew we'd probably want to hang out there for a week and we just didn't have the time.

The beginning of our drive was sad for me. It was difficult for me to reconcile the death of my grandmother with what she meant to me and my family. I loved her, certainly, but she was this weird entity that was holding me back. I could definitely see that now. This trip had opened my eyes, as had the burgeoning love and intimacy I felt with Maggie. So on the one hand I was distraught at my grandmother's passing. On the other, I felt much more liberated because of it. It was a weird dichotomy.

The scenery through Wyoming and then up into South Dakota was wild. The mountains tapered off and the terrain descended into flat grassland. And once we reached this beautiful prairie, we saw an insane number of antelope. I couldn't believe it. They were everywhere, on both sides of the road, just doing their thing. In defense of the antelope, there were very few cars driving on the road in this mostly desolate area. So desolate, in fact, at one point I saw a sign that read, "no gas station for 100 miles." That's how you know you're in the middle of nowhere.

But this drive gave Maggie and I an even greater opportunity to talk.

"Well, you know I was out in college," said Maggie. "It was never a big thing for me, I guess, and I count myself lucky for that. I come from a pretty artsy-fartsy family and it was never a question whether I could tell my parents on not. I mean, my aunt is a lesbian."

"When did you know?"

"When did I know?" said Maggie, looking over to me from the driver's side and smiling. "Immediately. Like, as soon as I started having sexual thoughts. I don't know. Maybe 12 or 13."

"You never felt like you were interested in guys?" I asked. "Not in high school or anything?"

"I definitely questioned it," said Maggie. "I thought about it. Because, you know, most of my friends were into guys. But I grew up in Oak Park, just outside of Chicago, and it's a pretty friendly place for us."

The way Maggie said "us" really made me feel included. It made me feel connected. It made me feel like I belonged.

"My grandmother was just pretty religious," I said. "And the way she sometimes talked about *the gays*, well, it made me feel shameful."

"Are your parents like that, too?"

"Not entirely," I said. "They're better than her. But I think it could be a little odd for them. I know they'd accept me. They love me unconditionally. They supported me through the whole separation and divorce. They just want me to be happy."

"It's sad," said Maggie. "But I'm optimistic. I know that I didn't have it nearly as hard as lesbian women did before me and I think the generation younger than us is going to have an even better time. I'm hopeful."

"Me too," I said with a smile.

"Gotta be," affirmed Maggie. We sat in comfortable silence for a moment as we drove down a long, straight road, prairie to either side. "So," said Maggie, breaking the silence. "Did you feel an attraction to women when you were younger, too?"

"Yeah," I admitted. "I did. I didn't know what to make of it, though, so I just stuffed it down."

"Was your hometown an accepting and tolerant place?"

"I don't know," I said. "Maybe not. I knew exactly one guy and one girl who were out. And they were kind of considered *freaks*, you know?"

"Oh, I know," said Maggie.

"I guess I just felt a lot of pressure to fit in. Fit in with the world around me, fit in with my family," I mused. "I ended up ignoring my feelings because they didn't fit the mold I was given."

"But it came back out in college," said Maggie happily with a sneaky grin. I laughed at her.

"Right," I said. "Lorna."

"*Lorna*," repeated Maggie in a dreamy and mocking sigh. She brought her hand up and fluffed out her own hair.

"Maybe my life would be entirely different if I had asked her out," I said.

"Could be," agreed Maggie. "But then again, maybe you wouldn't be here with me now." I looked to her, she looked to me, and we both smiled.

"That would suck," I said.

"Suck really bad," she said. "Things happen for a reason, I think."

"Yeah?" I said. "You believe in that sort of thing?"

"Definitely," said Maggie. "I believe the universe conspires to give you what you need, when you need it. That's the idea of karma."

"I thought karma was you do something shitty," I said, considering it. "And then something equally as shitty happens to you."

"Nope," she said. "Common misconception. It's not entirely cause and effect. That's just how we've sort of appropriated it."

"So what is it then?"

"Like I said," said Maggie. "When you need to see or experience something, whether good or bad, that's when the universe shows it to you. But it also, you know, is supposed to crossover from your past lives and all that so, um, I guess it's not a perfect explanation," she said winking.

"Ha," I said. "So take it with a grain of salt."

"That's up to you."

"Okay," I said. "So now that we've got that all established... how is it that I'm meant to only be able to come to these conclusions now?"

"I don't know!" beamed Maggie, shrugging, laughing. "I just think things come at the right time. Maybe if you'd hooked up with that Lorna chick, you would have had your heart broken and then went back to men anyway."

"Maybe."

"Anything's a possibility," she said. "I'm only saying... I'm pretty happy how this is unfolding *right now*. Can you agree with that?"

"I can agree," I said, flashing a glance over at her.

"Then we are in agreement!" confirmed Maggie, thrusting her finger into the air.

"Hands on the wheel, Mags."

"Right-o," she said, following my command. "I think you fit in now, doll," Maggie said after a moment. "I think you fit in nicely."

"I'm feeling that too," I smiled. "This is… it feels *nice* on me, you know?"

"Running from yourself is never the answer," she said. "You're only going to find pain down that road."

"I see that now."

"You're a sweetheart, Dana," said Maggie, a silly grin across her lips. I could tell she was smitten with me and that made me feel incredible. "I had no idea that this road trip would change my life so much. I thought you were just my friend. *A pretty good looking friend*, but… you know, just a friend." Sweet smile.

I sighed happily and just basked in the affirmation. It was good to feel wanted.

"I'm digging it, too," I said.

OUR NEXT STOP was Black Hills National Forest in South Dakota. Once the great plains ended, we traversed into the wonderful and lush lands of this scenic national treasure. Mountainous, opulent in its imposing wonder. Although the Black Hills had much to see, Mount Rushmore being one of the greatest stops, Maggie and I were beat from a long day of driving and wanted to find a suitable campsite.

We pulled into a heavily wooded area with a small parking lot. No other cars were around. Maggie eased the car into a far spot, put it in park, and shut the engine down. She just about melted into her seat after that, relaxing back into the leather, releasing an exasperated sigh.

"Dude, I am so tired," she said. "All this driving."

"We still have to pitch the tent," I said. "And figure out food."

"Figure out food?" she asked with a laugh. "Are you going to go hunt us an elk or something?"

"Yeah," I said teasingly. "Didn't you want elk burgers for dinner?"

"Well, we can't start a camp fire in this forest," she said, scrunching her nose up at me. "So good luck cooking it."

"I'm glad we picked up the extra large tub of hummus then," I grinned.

Maggie stuck her tongue out at me and unbuckled her seatbelt.

The tent Maggie had brought on the trip was quite fancy and easy to set up. In fact, in my time as a camper — which was, admittedly, very short — I'd never had such an easy time setting up a tent. We had walked a ways out from where we'd parked the car, deeper into the forest so that we couldn't really be seen from the main road, and to get a little bit of privacy.

We'd also brought a cooler out with us. Nothing huge, just a little red thing with enough food for the night and a six pack of beer. As Maggie had indicated creating a camp fire was off limits, but she had picked up a pretty nice lantern before the trip that would give us a good amount of light once the sun set.

As the afternoon transitioned into dusk, the temperature cooled down a lot. More than I'd expected for the middle of summer, actually. But we were, again, in the mountains at an elevation of near 5000 feet. I was glad to have brought a light jacket along.

With Maggie's lantern hanging from a nearby tree, the two of us sat on a couple of logs with a spread of veggies and cheese between us, building little sandwiches with woven wheat crackers, slurping happily from our beer cans. I have to admit that I was a bit trepidatious about camping. I'd done it before, sure, but not really in adulthood and I think I'd grown a little too soft as I waltzed into my 30s.

"This is a good beer," I said, looking at the can. "I rarely ever drink beer."

"Yeah," said Maggie, following my lead and looking at the can as well. "It's something local I guess."

"Is that going to be comfortable?" I asked, motioning with my head over to the tent. "I mean, like, am I going to feel every stick and rock underneath and get my back all jammed up?" Maggie laughed at me, shook her head, took another sip of beer.

"Yep," she jokingly affirmed. "You're going to feel every blade of grass, little miss *Princess and the Pea*."

"All right." I rolled my eyes very dramatically.

"C'mon," she said. "Camping is so not a big deal. We've

got a mattress pad in there. It's going to be comfortable enough. We're just roughing it a little bit."

"I can deal," I said, plunging a cut piece of celery into the tub of hummus.

"I do have to admit camping isn't the same without a fire," Maggie weighed in, looking toward the lantern longingly. "We'll have to go to my family's cabin up in Minnesota sometime. Then we can do the whole camp fire thing. It's on a lake, too."

"I'd love that," I said, happily smiling over at her. "What's it like up there?"

"Quiet," she said. "Private. It's way out there. It's near the Canadian border."

"Wow," I said. "I bet it gets cold."

"Uh, *heck yeah*," said Maggie. "But in the summer, like right now, it's amazing. The lake is totally underpopulated and pristine. Just an amazing spot."

"Next year," I grinned.

"Next year," Maggie agreed.

By the time we opened up our second cans of beer, I was starting to feel a bit relaxed and loopy. It was nice. Darkness had surrounded us in the forest, though the we had the lantern to light our conversation. We were laughing together, joking, having a great time and getting closer. But we also hit on more serious notes. Maggie had always been special to me but she was becoming something far more. I was eager to know what might happen to us when we returned to Chicago.

"Well!" said Maggie, weighing my question. "My hope is that this will, *uh*, continue. Does that sound about right?"

"It does." I couldn't suppress my smile, I was buzzing with wonderful feelings. "So does that mean that I have my first girlfriend?" This gave Maggie such a laugh, she almost fell off her log.

"You're so funny, Dana," she said. "Yes, I think you have your first girlfriend."

"My grandmother would be so proud," I said with a straight face.

"That gallows humor…" said Maggie, getting serious, holding a finger up and pointing it at me. She looked very straight as well. Then she broke. "…is hilarious and I support it 100%."

"It's how some of us cope."

"And others of us help the bereaved cope with our fingers and tongues," said Maggie devilishly. I could see the light in her eyes.

"Is that right?" I said like I was being enlightened to a secret. "Hmm. I think I could get used to those benefits."

We laughed together. My heart raced as I thought about Maggie and our budding relationship. Before I knew it, Maggie had stood up from her log, beer can in hand, and moseyed over toward me. She sat down next to me on my log.

"Hi," she said sweetly.

"Hi."

Then we were kissing and it was awesome. I felt a warmth boil up in my belly. Together, both Maggie and I closed our eyes softly and sighed into one another's lips. I could feel my heart rate ramp up, my legs wobble. It was as though we were in our own private little world. Out there in the wilderness, surrounded by forest, by darkness, by the sounds of insect nightlife and the occasional far-off howl. I'd be just fine if we never went back home again, if we turned the car around and just kept driving west like we both wanted to do. I had quit my old life, so I might as well send everything else packing with it. My job, my apartment, my life in Chicago. Maggie represented the future to me and the future most certainly looked bright.

Later on, I had already snuggled up into my sleeping bag inside of the tent with the lantern stuffed into one corner, the light dimmed. I sighed happily, I smiled, I kicked my feet a little bit as I waited for Maggie to get back. I couldn't believe I was feeling so enthused about a new relationship at 35 years old. But at the same time, this felt like the first time I was getting involved in someone I truly longed for. It wasn't just some ruse, it wasn't me feeling like I had some duty to fulfill. This was about fun, about happiness.

Outside the tent, through the thin material, I saw a flashlight's beam bouncing toward me. It grew closer and closer until the light shined into the tent through the open door flap and then Maggie poked her head in.

"Got room for one more?" she asked with a grin.

"Of course."

"Great," she said. Flicking off the flashlight, she crawled inside the tent and zipped the flap closed. Maggie then slipped out of her flip-flops and maneuvered around, unbuttoning her jeans and beginning to slide out of them.

"All the food okay?" I asked.

"Everything's in the car," she said. "Don't want to have any visitors to our campsite in the middle of the night."

"Right."

Underneath Maggie's jeans she had on a simple black pair of panties and now, on her hands and knees, wearing just her underwear and a tank top, she began fussing with her sleeping bag to get it open so she could get inside it for the night. Once inside, Maggie slithered her hand behind her back, unhooked her bra, and pulled it out from under her tank top.

"It's like a song out there," I mused softly, my eyes focused on her as she got situated in her sleeping bag. "All those chirps and creeks and whatever else."

"It's beautiful," said Maggie. "I love the sound of nature. It's much better than all the yelling and sirens we hear in the city."

"And fireworks at odd hours," I said with a laugh.

"Yeah, those too."

"I've got to admit to you, Maggie," I said. "It's not bad in here. I'm pretty comfortable."

"I knew you would be," she said. "Hey," said Maggie, bringing her arm out of her bag and deftly unzipping the side of it. "Want to get close?"

"I do," I said. I followed her lead, unzipped the side of my sleeping bag so that we had an opening between us. As I did this, Maggie reached over to the side of the tent and grabbed a fleece blanket, tossing it over top of the both of us. Then we worked together to get closer, arms sneaking in to the other's bags, warmly touching accepting bodies.

"Mmm," she groaned softly, reaching her hand up and removing her glasses. Maggie folded the arms into the frames and set them off to the side. "Do you prefer me with or without my glasses?" she asked, smiling sweetly.

"I think you're equally pretty either way."

"A very political answer," Maggie said. Leaning toward me, she pressed her lips into mine and we kissed. I felt a wave of wonderment wash over me. Squirming a bit under the blanket, under the sleeping bag, I tried to get even closer to her, feeling her slim body underneath all that material. With help from the warmth between us, I dissolved into our sensual kiss. I was eager to be next to her. My hands explored up and down her small figure.

As we kissed, I dropped my hands down to her butt and gave her cheeks each a firm squeeze at the same time. I adored squeezing her ass. It was so nice and full. As I did this, Maggie flexed her cheeks to make them feel even more solid, more strong.

"Not bad, huh?" she murmured between kisses.

"Very good," I countered, adoringly feeling her rump. Excited for more, I threaded both of my hands into the elastic band of her panties and slipped fingers first down inside. Her rear was a little cold but it started to warm as my hands rubbed over it.

"That's nice," Maggie cooed against my mouth. Her hands snuck under my t-shirt at my waist, lovingly massaging my love handles, offering up firm squeezes just as I did to her butt. I, too, was dressed down to my underwear and I could feel that familiar trickle in my middle as my arousal mounted.

"I've never fooled around in a tent before," I admitted through humid breath.

"First time for everything," said Maggie, eager to return to kissing, to return to touching.

It wasn't much longer until Maggie plunged a hand down the front of my panties, her fingertips running through my fur, and easing down further still until she suddenly touched me where I loved it, sending a quick electric chill through my body. I shivered and I sighed, body vibrating, almost grunting as I kissed her harder. Her hand began pumping back and forth, fingers rubbing over my slit, offering me a firm massage as the tensile fabric of my panties kept her hand close.

Pulling my hands out from the back of Maggie's underwear, I began to push my own over my butt and down my thighs to give Maggie greater access to me. As soon as I did this, my panties hanging at my knees, Maggie really increased her speed, pressing back and forth between my lips, often moving her fingertips upward to caress my clit, then eagerly returning to my wetness to inspire an ever increasingly lust within me.

The sounds from outside of our tent, the insects, the various forest creatures, it was almost as though they had gone silent. All I could hear were the heated and stumbling breaths coming from both Maggie and I, alongside the light zippy commotion of sleeping bags rubbing together.

"Oh God," I said reflexively, my head collapsing downward against Maggie's shoulder. Maggie had penetrated me, easily slipping two fingers inside of me, slowly and methodically pulling them out only to immediately push them back in again. With each pressured push, I felt her palm slip up against my wanting little pink bean, the movements of her moistened hand giving me a case of the quivers.

Maggie was an expert at fingering. My experience with past lovers left something to be desired. Who would have thought that someone who possessed the same parts as you did would know their way around, right? I adored the steady pressure of Maggie's thrusts and I grinded up against her as though I were riding her fingers. I tried to resume kissing her a few more times but the pleasure made it a bit too difficult to focus. Instead I simply cradled up against her and enjoyed the attention.

Moving her fingers out of me, Maggie pressed her fingertips against my bud and massaged in slow, steady circles. I gripped onto her and convulsed, mechanically jerking forward against her as the jolts of desire coursed through me.

"Keep doing that," I sighed against her ear and she obeyed without hesitation. Maggie continued her circles as she buried her face into my neck and tenderly kissed me. I felt my thighs squeeze inward automatically, which I then tried to counter with forced relaxation. Each time I did that, however, my legs would automatically clench soon after against Maggie's diddling hand.

The two of us shifted together underneath the mess of sleeping bags and blankets, clamoring for each other, lust drunk and eager to absorb the heat between us. Even though I was the one being touched, Maggie herself was releasing soft little moans along with her breath, indicating her enjoyment and her arousal by the hot mingling of our desire. I felt the pressure building inside and I reveled in it. I was so jazzed up, I felt as though my heart was about to rip out of my chest. My breath was short, the time between my reflexive clenches and releases even shorter.

"I'm gonna come," I whispered to Maggie. "Don't stop, okay?"

"Okay," she called back breathily.

I felt it start in my belly, my body slowly building to a quiver. Soon my toes and my fingertips felt numb, I felt cold, my butt started to wiggle, my thighs quaking. Then I gripped hard to Maggie, holding her tightly as my body jerked around, her hand pressing against my wet mound, matted fur against my flesh, just cupping me gently as my orgasm began to overtake me. I was moaning into Maggie's ear, gritting my teeth, groaning, whining. I felt love overtake me and a huge tidal wave of emotion burst over me. And Maggie, too, held me. One hand between my thighs, the other at my side. She adoringly comforted me as I came.

"Oh shit," I whispered, eyes clenched tight, almost crying. It was spectacular. I was so happy, I think I was drooling.

And then Maggie was shushing me, lightly running her fingers through my hair, comforting me, kissing me. All the pleasure I had felt wash over me continued it's movement until I started giggling. I couldn't help it. I was joyfully giggling. It just was magical.

"Did that do the trick?" Maggie asked with the familiar teasing timbre in her voice.

"It's still... you know," I said, searching for the words. "It's still going." My body shivered and my limbs wagged, all beyond my control.

"I love doing that to you," said Maggie. "You look so happy afterwards."

"Oh yeah?" I said. "Why would I be anything else?"

"I don't know!" replied Maggie. "I just like seeing that happiness on your face."

"Thank you," I said evenly. I placed a soft, sweet kiss on her lips. "Mmm. I feel all tingly."

"That's how I like you, babe," she said, kissing me now. We exchanged audible kisses a few more times. "Tingly and happy."

I felt as though I were living a dream. Intertwined there amid the rumpled sleeping bags, limbs woven, bare leg to bare leg, arms wrapped around one another, I was just so infatuated with Maggie. I kissed her cheek, I kissed her forehead. She had put a spell on me and I was loving it. The two of us gazed into one another's eyes and I reveled at how deep blue hers were, blue with little specks. I don't know if I just hadn't noticed it before, but Maggie had a smattering of little freckles at the bridge of her nose. I loved each one of those freckles. I wanted to kiss them all individually. I wanted to admire them forever.

I wanted to wake up each morning and see Maggie smiling contentedly beside me. Every morning from then until eternity.

———

HAND IN HAND, Maggie and I slowly sauntered up the long stone walkway, tall pillars on either side with the various state flags flying atop them, large trees beyond the pillars. As we walked past these pillars, each labeled with the corresponding state name and year admitted to the union emblazoned on the side, together we each searched for what we knew the other was also looking for.

"Bam!" said Maggie suddenly, pointing and then leaping over, pulling me along with her. "Found it. Illinois, the 21st state, admitted in 1818!"

"Fine, fine," I said, rolling my eyes. "You found it first. Let's just get to the monument already. I can see it from here," I said, now pointing my finger out toward the huge mountain in front of us. And into that mountain was carved four heads, each looking regal and stoic. This was Mount Rushmore, one of the most iconic national monuments in the United States. It was large and imposing and unlike anything I'd ever seen before. Yet there Maggie was, gawking over a stone pillar with our home state chiseled into it.

"It was a competition, Dana," said Maggie, clearly

explaining it to me. "A contest. And, as it turns out, I won that contest."

"C'mon," I said, yanking at her hand and pulling her along. Maggie laughed excitedly and closed in on me, the two of us lightly smacking hips.

"We gotta see the presidents!" barked Maggie, still laughing. "Out of our way!"

"Shh!" I said, suddenly feeling embarrassed but absolutely loving it. "Stop being a goof."

"You don't *really* want me to stop being a goof," she said. "Do you?"

"I don't."

"I knew it."

The monument was absolutely packed. Mostly with families. Just a ton of people wandering around, taking pictures, trying to find their own state pillar just as we had, admiring the grandeur of this place. As Maggie and I neared the end of the walkway, we looked down and saw an amphitheater below the mountain. But above, etched into the mountainside were the visages of Washington, Jefferson, Roosevelt, and Lincoln. It was crazy to see such a sight. I'd never seen a sculpture so large before.

"It's smaller than I thought it would be," mused Maggie.

"Are you kidding me?"

"Half kidding," she said, grinning. Her glasses scooted up her nose.

"Have you ever seen anything like this before?" I said, motioning toward it. "It's nuts. Say what you want about the politics of any of these guys, it's just pretty insane to see peoples' faces carved this large in a huge granite mountainside."

"Okay," affirmed Maggie. "You're right. I've never seen a granite sculpture this big. So that's cool."

"You don't sound very impressed," I said.

"I mean, I *am*," she said, thinking about it. "Or, I *want* to be. Maybe I've just seen so many pictures of it, like it's so ingrained in my memory, that it feels like I've actually already been here before."

"Have you been here before?" I said. "With your family or something?"

"Nope," said Maggie. "Never. Look, it's definitely *cool* Dana." Maggie was getting animated, pointing out toward the mountain. Meanwhile groups of people walked up to either side of us as we debated, snapping photos, posing in front of the graven image before us.

"But?"

"But nothing," she said. "That's it. Check it off the list."

"You're just hilarious," I said, shaking my head. "Well I, for one, am glad we came to see it."

"I'm *glad*," said Maggie, slinking an arm around my waist and pulling herself close to me. "I'm glad I got to see it with you."

"Okay," I said, putting my arm around her shoulders. "You get a pass."

"They could have at least finished that side of Abe's face," she said, pointing up.

"Maybe you could pitch that to the park," I said. "Heck,

maybe you can get up there and do the carving. You're an artist, after all."

"I could probably do that," said Maggie in mock seriousness, nodding as she considered it. "But maybe next summer."

"I thought we were going to Minnesota next summer?"

"Fine, the summer after that," she said.

"We'll see."

Although I was definitely excited to see Mount Rushmore, the longer we stood there the more I thought Maggie was right. It was undeniably cool but after looking at it for a couple of minutes, well, you've seen it. It's sort of one of those bucket list things I guess, one of the modern wonders you need to see and then probably never see again. How many people have gone to Mount Rushmore multiple times?

"Maybe if they have events down there at the amphitheater," remarked Maggie as we walked down that stone corridor and back toward the entrance. "I mean, if you live around here and they do presentations, maybe you come here once a month. I don't know!"

"Did you notice what the woman at the parking lot booth said?" I asked. "The parking pass was good for the entire year."

"Ha, yeah, that made me laugh inside," said Maggie. "Oh great, I'll just slip this into my glove compartment for when I come back here within 12 months." The two of us laughed together.

A comfortable silence overtook us, the two of us walking, holding hands, oblivious to all the people running around. I felt like it was so easy to talk to Maggie, to joke with her. We had this connection. We had an unspoken thing. It made me undeniably happy.

"When we get back to Chicago," I said, speaking up through the break in conversation. "Can we spend a lot of time together?"

"Next thing you know," said Maggie. I could tell she was setting up a tease. "You're going to want to move in together. Dana, you *are* a lesbian."

"Is that a thing?" I asked. "I don't get it."

"It's a joke," said Maggie. "It's just a stereotype that lesbians move in together fast."

"Well, I *am* month to month on the lease at my place," I said, playing along.

"You can move in if I can just keep you in my bedroom," said Maggie. "Stripped down bare, just ready and waiting to please me when I get home from work."

"That can be arranged," I grinned. Leaning in closer to her, I placed a sweet kiss on the side of her head.

"Aw," she cooed. "Thanks."

"Hey Mags," I said, tapping my fingers into her hand as we held hands and walked.

"Yes, babe?"

"Am I bitch for not wanting to be home for my grand-mother's funeral?"

"Are you a bitch?" she repeated, giving me kind of a silly and confused look.

"Yeah," I admitted candidly. I spoke with a heavy heart, with a sense of worry and dread, but I felt like I could truly open up to Maggie and that she would be able to give me great advice. "You know, I feel like I *should* want to race home, even though my mother told me that it wasn't necessary. She's being cremated, it's just going to be a service around her urn. I just... I don't think I really even care to be there."

"And you think that makes you a bitch?" she asked.

"Yeah."

"I think it just makes you human," said Maggie. "Your grandmother, well, she wasn't really there for you throughout your life. Right?"

"Right," I said. "I mean, I always felt distant from her. From her opinions."

"And it's not like you totally neglected her from, like, a family standpoint... right?" Maggie said, raising her brow. "You visited her often when she was in the nursing home."

"That's right," I affirmed. "I talked to her, I tried to be positive, I did my best."

"I think you're putting too much pressure on yourself to be perfect," she said. "You being at the funeral isn't going to bring your grandmother back from the dead and it isn't going to change the fact that she's pretty much responsible for you hiding from yourself for so long."

I took a deep breath and then audibly sighed.

"Look," said Maggie, stopping, turning toward me. She had a beaming smile on her face. Her eyes glimmered through the lenses of her stylish glasses. I loved her eyebrows. They there thick and full. Maggie's face just enthralled me. It was pretty and it was so kind.

"Yeah?" I peeped, weakly smiling back.

"This is all we got," she said, opening her arms up. "Right now. That's it. Would it be preferable that you were back home and easily able to go to the funeral? Sure. Or, maybe not. But that doesn't matter. We're half way across the country, we're having a ton of fun together," Maggie said, grinning, demurely looking down for a moment. I could tell she was elated by what was going on between us. "We're here now. We've got a mountain of presidents staring over us!" she exclaimed, now wagging a hand toward Mount Rushmore, still in view.

"True," I said.

"I'm just saying, Dana *Darling*," Maggie continued, happily grinning. "This is great. Our trip is coming to an end, sure, but *this*..." she said, motioning back and forth between the two of us. "This is really just beginning."

I couldn't help myself. I leapt forward and wrapped my arms around Maggie, pulling her in for a tight embrace. Her positivity, her love, her light, that's what I needed at this point in my life. And she was so willing to give it. We stood there hugging for a few moments, silent and content, until we both pulled back and simultaneously came in for a kiss. I'd been searching for this kind of affection for a long time.

"So what's next?" I asked finally.

"Hmm," mused Maggie, pressing her finger into the corner of her lip. "I think I've got an idea."

"Huh," I remarked, walking into the storefront after Maggie. While she excitedly jaunted inside, I slowly ambled, looking around, trying to take it all in. It was kind of a ramshackle store, with florescent lights above, a concrete floor. It was filled with tables and boxes, the walls lined with displays. And although the store itself could use a bit of upkeep, the wares they sold were all quite beautiful. It was a rock and gem shop and I honestly never knew such a place existed.

"I love rocks," admitted Maggie, grinning back at me as I followed her. "Did you know I collect them?"

"Is that why you wanted to go on this mountain road trip?"

"Precisely!" she said. "I hope it's not too boring looking through all these with me — *ooh! Chrysocolla!*" Interrupting herself, Maggie turned toward a display and began sorting through a box of greenish-blue stones.

"They are pretty," I admitted, watching Maggie as she picked up the rocks one at a time, held them, looked them over, and put them back down again.

"I've been taking a jewelry making class at my college," she said. "As a professor, I can take up to two free classes a semester if I like. So yeah, I'm taking this jewelry class, learning how to do that, and some of these stones would be *perfect* for a necklace or something. Look!" Maggie held up a small but glittering stone, wavy green, little coppery lines haphazard throughout.

"Nice," I smiled.

"You don't care," she said teasingly, yanking the stone

175

back and continuing to look through the bin. "Rocks, rocks, rocks," Maggie sung to herself as she dug.

"I do so," I said. "I care about your interests. I mean, I care about you and want you to be happy. If this makes you happy… that's awesome."

"It definitely does," she said without looking up. "And we should all do the things that make us happy regardless of what anybody else thinks." With that, Maggie looked up to me and grinned. I loved the way her lips turned when she grinned, the little crinkles at the corners of her mouth.

"You're relating it back to me," I said. I caught on quickly.

"You're a perceptive lady," Maggie said. "I'm just trying to prepare you," she said, continuing her walk through the store and I dutifully followed her. "You know when we get back home people are going to have a *lot* of questions for you if you bring me around."

"I hadn't really considered that yet," I mused, feeling slightly heavy from the revelation.

"A woman in her mid-30s, considered straight by everyone she knows — including her family — comes back from a cross country trip, bumping vag with a feisty pocket-sized blonde," said Maggie, posing like a model as she referenced herself. "I mean, your tongue is going to get an even greater work out than it has on this trip."

"That's a pretty funny joke," I admitted.

"I know."

"I guess I hadn't really thought of it like that," I said.

"But I had a gut feeling something rough was lingering behind the next door."

"Maybe everybody will be like, 'Dana? Oh yeah, I knew she was a lesbian way before even *she* knew,'" said Maggie. "But I'm a pretty good judge of character and I didn't have any idea. You hid it well."

"Hmm," I said, tapping my finger to my chin.

"You just have to own it," said Maggie, laying it out for me as she dug through another box of gemstones. We were now in the middle of the store, near the register, as a woman in her 60s lingered around behind the counter. "I had this girlfriend one time," she said. "Super cool chick, kind hearted, but pretty wholesome in a lot of ways and definitely... um... *conservative* in the bedroom."

"Okay," I said slowly.

"And you know now that I, to put it frankly, like butt stuff," said Maggie. "I don't think it's weird and I don't like to be shamed because I enjoy it. I think that's messed up."

"I hope that I haven't shamed you for—"

"No," said Maggie, looking at me over the top of her glasses, holding up a palm. "Not you. This chick, this ex-girlfriend. She thought I was *brainwashed* or something. She thought that some ex-*boyfriend*, some *man*, had brainwashed me into thinking that anal sex was okay. I told her, 'babe, I've *never* been with a man. I like this because I like it, end of story.'"

"What did she say?"

"She couldn't believe it. She couldn't believe that something she found weird — something she was *unwilling* to even try — wasn't something that another woman like her could enjoy," said Maggie, shrugging her shoulders and tossing her hands up. "What the fuck? If you're a prude, that's on you. Don't try to spoil *my* good time or make me feel *less* than you for engaging in something I like!"

"That makes sense," I said. "Who cares if you like it? What difference does it make?"

"Right," she said. "But, well, it doesn't quite make a sexual relationship work if you want her to slip a finger up your tush and she thinks you're from a different planet."

"I can see that," I said, letting the smile wash over my face, trying to push down a laugh.

"All I'm saying is that you've got to own it," said Maggie, smiling wide as she saw my amusement. "Just be you. And do it with a smile."

"I agree," said a voice off to the side. Maggie and I both turned our heads and saw the woman behind the counter, her hair gray and long and straight, a bit of a hippie vibe, wearing a busy cardigan sweater. "I can admit I like a finger in my rear and I don't care who knows it."

Maggie's eyes grew wide and I knew she wanted to laugh. Not laugh at the woman, of course, but laugh at the situation. I could read it loud and clear on her face. It was absurd and Maggie thrived in the absurd.

"I like your style!" said Maggie finally, pointing emphatically at the woman.

"Oh my God," I said, grinning, looking down, shaking my head. "I can't believe she overheard us."

"Don't be embarrassed, dear," said the woman. "I didn't

mean to interrupt your conversation. I just wanted to let you know I'm with you."

"Thank you," I said, definitely feeling embarrassed. "I appreciate it."

"I just can't believe some people *care* about what other people do in the privacy of their own bedroom," said Maggie, engaging the woman. "Am I right?"

"Right," said the woman. "There's nothing that gets me going better than when my husband goes down on me and fiddles around with my backside. It just feels good."

"It does," agreed Maggie firmly. "It feels really good. We're not weird, ma'am, we're perfectly fine."

"I don't need to be convinced," I said. "I've done it, I like it, we're all on the same team here."

"We're just having a conversation," grinned Maggie. "It's not to convince any of us. We're just commiserating on why it's stupid to worry about what others think, why it's important to be yourself. You see, ma'am," said Maggie, now talking to the woman behind the counter. "My girl-friend here is going to have to open up to some people once she gets back home and—" she said, then interrupted herself with a little gasps. "Is that picture jasper?" She pointed into the glass case in front of us.

"It is!" said the woman.

"Ooh!" beamed Maggie. "Let me see!"

Although I felt highly embarrassed to talk about some-thing so intimate with a total stranger, there was something amazingly comfortable in the back and forth with Maggie, something I appreciated for what it was. Some of us, even with a best friend or lover or a lover who's also your best friend, can find it difficult to open up about the most private things inside ourselves. I knew that had always been the case with me and my relationships. But I was blessed to have found Maggie. She had no filters in that regard. Whether because she had always just been open and honest or because she was tired of maintaining that wall between people, she would just simply say what she thought and not give a damn if you judged her for it. It was refreshing. In a world of people hiding their ulterior motives and judgments, with Maggie what you saw was what you got.

"Okay, gimme this one," said Maggie, sliding one of the stones off to the side. She and the woman had shifted gears, talking now about stones like they had never even broached the topic of anal sex. It was hard to believe but then at the same time, knowing Maggie, it really wasn't.

I just smiled and watched, the embarrassment draining out of me. Serenity flowed over me.

Maggie was right. Of course she was. You can't let the opinions of others dictate your happiness. Nobody is going to like everything about you. Well, maybe you'll get lucky and find a woman like Maggie. But let's be real. It's just fantasy to think everything is going to be just how you like it, that other people are going to fit into nice little boxes to accommodate whatever it is that *you* like. It's lunacy. That's why it's so crazy that I let the overbearing matriarch of my family run my life for as long as she did. That's why I should have no fears about going home and living my life in the freedom I deserve.

So what if I spent my entire life dating men, even going as far as to marry and subsequently divorce one? That's my past. And that's over with. If I learned anything on this road trip with Maggie, it's that there's no reason to hide from my feelings. Nothing *truly* bad is going to happen. In fact, bad stuff will probably only happen the longer you hide from your feelings. It's like the pathological liar who has to keep coming up with new and associated lies to keep their previous lies afloat. Sooner or later it's all going to come tumbling down. And then what? That's a lot of rebuilding you'd have to do.

That's sort of where I was at, I guess. But I was ready to leave that life behind and see what was waiting for me on the other side. The side where I didn't have to lie. The side where I didn't have to feel like a deer in the headlights every time I was discussing my love life with someone. Having to play along, talk about what I wanted in a man, have friends try to set me up or whatever. That was such a hard ruse to keep up. It just wasn't worth it.

I was ready, firmly planted in adulthood, to really start living for myself.

"That's right," said Maggie, listening as the woman dressed in a suit jacket behind the counter spoke to her. We were in the lobby of a pretty nice hotel, just outside of Madison, Wisconsin. Although we probably could have soldiered on and drove home to Chicago, I don't think either of us were quite ready to admit that our trip was coming to an end. It had been so fun, so liberating, and it was unthinkable that it could almost be over.

"I have a room available with two queen sized beds," said the woman, tapping into her computer.

"Do you have one with just one king?" said Maggie.

"Let me see." Her fingers clacked over her keyboard. "We do and that room is $199 per night."

"Book it!" said Maggie, hosting a finger into the air. "Maybe we should hang out in Madison for a few days," she said to me, smiling ear to ear. "It's a cool town."

"I've got to get back to work on Monday," I mourned.

"I suppose I should, too," said Maggie. "No students yet but still so much to do."

"Do you have a credit card we can keep on file?" asked the woman, eyebrows lifted.

"I do," said Maggie, sliding her card across the counter. The woman smiled, took it, and returned to her computer screen.

"Thank you."

"This trip, though," I said. "I wish I could extend it forever."

"In a way we can," Maggie said with an irrepressible smile. Reaching over, she took my hand and played with my fingers.

"I think so." I smiled back. I couldn't help it.

"All right, Ms. Stack," said the woman, sliding Maggie's card back to her. "You're all set for one night here at the Winston. I'll give the both of you a key card." Reaching across the counter, she handed both Maggie and I cards for the room. "Room 527, the fifth floor."

"Thanks," we said in unison.

"Is there a restaurant here in the hotel?" I asked.

"There is," she said. "Just around this corner here," said the woman, half leaning across the desk and pointing. "Across from the elevator bank. You can't miss it. It's a seafood restaurant. If you like sea bass, I recommend giving that a try. It's very good."

"Great," I said.

"So we're all set?" asked Maggie.

"All set, ma'am," said the woman. "Enjoy your stay."

With bags in hand, Maggie and I sashayed through the lobby and made our way toward the elevator. The hotel was fancy, in a modern sort of way, and it was a big leap from the accommodations we had been staying in.

"I can give you some cash for the room," I said as Maggie leaned out and pressed the button to call the elevator.

"Forget about it," she said. "It was my idea to go ritzy for the last night of our trip. I got you, doll."

"Thanks." I kissed her cheek.

"You know the best part of staying in a hotel?" Maggie said with a hint of fire in her eyes. I knew she was about to say something inappropriate or otherwise crack a joke.

"I'm not sure I want to know," I said.

"Hotel sex," she said matter-of-factly. "It's different from any other sex because you just don't give a damn about the room. You're free to get wild with it." I laughed and shook my head.

"Yeah, but then that's what *everybody* thinks," I said as we stepped into the open elevator together. "So hotel rooms, I mean, they've got to be pretty gross."

"They change the sheets!" Maggie protested, the elevator door now closing behind us.

"Not the bed spread," I countered. "Not the curtains."

"The curtains?" she sputtered. "I don't know what kind of sick stuff *you're* into, Dana." Maggie paused for effect. "But count me in!"

LATER ON, the two of us sat opposite each other at the hotel restaurant. We had just been delivered fresh glasses of wine and were awaiting our desert. A few other people were also in attendance, some lone business travelers, some couples like us just passing through, but it was a fairly quiet night for the restaurant. The lights were low, the ambience was calming. I was smiling. I was smiling a lot lately and it felt good.

"I like this," I said as I watched Maggie take a sip of her wine. "This feels like a real date." She almost did a spit take, chortling from my revelation.

"Yeah?" she said, wiping her mouth with her clothe napkin. "So the past few weeks, all those meals we had, all those times I licked your cooter, those weren't dates?"

"Don't call it a cooter."

"I'll call it whatever I want, love," she said, now taking another drink from her glass.

"Well, I mean, they were different," I mused. "I don't know. This is just a nice restaurant, a fancy meal. It feels very relaxing."

"You're right," Maggie said in earnest. "I can admit, this feels like a date. It's nice."

"It is," I agreed.

"I have to tell you, Dana," she said. "No playing around. I'm being serious. This feels awesome. Like hands down, so special, like nothing I've ever experienced before. I never thought in a million years that this would happen to us." Maggie shook her head as she thought about it. Her face had grown serious.

"It's like a dream," I said. "I sure as hell hope it's not a dream."

"Pinch me," she insisted, sticking her arm across the table. I humored her and pinched her. "Not a dream," she confirmed. We both laughed.

"I know I've got a lot to think about," I said. "A lot on my mind. A lot to deal with when we get back to Chicago. But Maggie, I'm just... I'm so grateful for you and I'm so happy that this happened for us."

"I feel the same way," she said. "This just feels right, you know? It feels like it was meant to happen."

"It really does."

"And it's kind of a fairy tale right now, I can admit," Maggie said, tilting her glass back and forth as she considered her words. "It probably won't be all buttercups and rainbows, because we're kind of living this weird fantasy vacation life at the moment where everything is peachy keen."

"Agreed," I said.

"But… I don't care," she said with a smile. "To be able to take your friend, someone who you get along with so well, someone who you go back so far with, someone you've always loved… to take them and convert them into your romantic partner," Maggie almost got choked up as she spoke. "It's cool," she said firmly. "It's just really fucking cool."

"You're cool," I said, pointing at her, trying to put on a stereotypically 'cool' face. Maggie laughed.

"That's a little geeky," she teased.

"Can I share something with you?" I said, suddenly feeling nervous. I let my mouth go into autopilot because I knew I wanted to get what I was about to say off my chest, but I was still trepidatious about revealing it.

"Of course," Maggie said. "You can tell me anything."

"All right," I replied, looking off. I exhaled and then smiled at her. "Remember at the beginning of our trip? At that AirBnB in Omaha?"

"I remember," Maggie said happily. "I was there."

"This is going to sounds crazy," I said. "But when we shared a bed that night… I…" I paused and took a moment, unsure how to get the words out. "I got myself off thinking about you."

"What!" said Maggie, her smile growing even wider. She

couldn't help herself and she smacked the table, causing the silverware to clank. "You did that?"

"I did."

"Oh my God," she said. "That's hilarious."

"You don't think I'm a creep?" I asked sheepishly.

"You're *definitely* a creep," she said. "But I love it. That's so perfect."

"I just had to tell you," I said. "I'd been feeling weird about it and I'm glad I could get it off my chest."

"My only regret is that you didn't wake me up and let me join in," said Maggie. "We could have raced."

"Something tells me you'd win that race," I said with a relieved grin. It felt good to admit it to Maggie.

"Okay, my turn," she said, straightening up in her chair, taking another sip of wine. Maggie didn't look guilty of anything at all. She seemed excited.

"I don't know if I'm ready."

"Well, get ready," she said. "Back in college, when we lived together…"

"Yeah…"

"Sophomore year, right?"

"Right."

"One weekend when you went home," said Maggie. "I tried on, like, all your panties."

"You didn't," I said, shaking my head, unable to stop the smile curling onto my lips. "I should be so mad at you. That's so crazy."

"I know," said Maggie gleefully. "I know it is. But you

had this cute pair that I always liked and I tried those on first. Then I just couldn't stop myself."

"That is *weird*, Maggie," I said. "That's weird."

"I've always had trouble with boundaries," she said smirking.

"I can't believe you're telling me this at this fancy restaurant," I said. I let out a chuckle. I was blown away by the absurdity.

"You masturbated in the same bed as me, like, two weeks ago or whatever!" Maggie protested, her words coming out a little too loud.

"Okay, okay," I said, putting my hands up, trying to quiet her down. She craned her neck to look around, realizing she indeed might have been talking too loud.

"This was 15 years ago," Maggie said. "I should get a pass."

"I'm not mad," I said through a laugh. "It doesn't matter. It's a funny story now. But you must admit that it's weird."

"I admit it," she said. "You forgive me?"

"Of course."

"Thanks," she said cutely.

"Here comes desert," I said in a whisper. "Shh!"

Just then, our waiter approached the table with a reserved smile. He placed a single plate between us upon which was a warm chocolate brownie, thick as hell, topped with an overlarge scoop of vanilla ice cream that had already begun melting down the side of the confection.

"Ladies," he said. "Here we have the molten brownie a

la mode. Enjoy." He bowed slightly and made himself scarce.

"Oh my," said Maggie, looking down into the desert and reaching for her desert spoon. "Oh my, oh my, oh my."

"Delectable," I said, following Maggie's lead and readying myself to dig in. "I don't think this meal could get any better."

"I think it can," said Maggie, looking up at me, her blue eyes dancing.

———

THE SHEETS on our bed where a mess, torn asunder, the bedspread collected in a heap down on the floor. The light in the room was low and warm, only the two lamps on either side of the bed lit. I lay there naked, legs spread, the wetness between them beginning to evaporate as my chest heaved up and down. My hairline felt sweaty, as did my lower back, and underneath my knees. My belly rose and then it fell. I could still feel the little judders of orgasm travel through me, tiny pulses of energy, wonderful pleasure.

I lowered my hand and caressed myself, my own creaminess sticking lightly to my fingers as I tenderly petted. I was eager for more. Being with Maggie had opened me up sexually, in more ways than one, and I longed for her to return from the bathroom and resume touching me.

Maggie was right. Hotel sex *was* a different kind of sex.

I heard the door to the bathroom pop open and I looked across the room. Maggie sashayed out, a spring in her step. She was dancing, one foot in front of the other, grinning happily. Her blonde hair was tied back in a loose bun, she was topless, her breasts softly jiggling as she moved. Maggie still wore her panties, beige shiny satin with strawberries emblazoned on them, but I noticed something odd. There was a huge bulge underneath the fabric. Her dancing was designed to accentuate the bulge, like she was showing off.

"What the hell is that?" I asked. I placed a hand on my upper chest, still collecting my breath.

"This ol' thing?" Maggie said casually. Reaching down, she pushed her hand into her underwear and yanked out the bulge, holding it up for me to see. It was a very familiar looking purple silicon dildo.

"No," I said.

"Yes," she countered.

"You took that thing from that girl's place in Salt Lake City?"

"You know it," Maggie said, grinning wide, inspecting the toy. "I figured we should have a keepsake from our trip, a little reminder of the sprouting of our relationship."

Maggie waltzed over to me and sat down on the side of the bed.

"I can't believe you," I said.

"Relax," she replied. "I sent her a message apologizing."

"Yeah, how did that go?"

"Well, I just told her that as a joke my drunk friend hid her, *um*, device…" said Maggie with a wildness in her face. "Hid it in my toiletry bag and we drove off with it. I told her

I'd send her some money to cover the cost. She thought it was funny."

"I'm going to have to watch you like a hawk," I said. "If I don't keep my eyes on you, you're going to get us in a lot of trouble."

"I think you enjoy my whimsical ways," she said, lowering the toy to me, guiding it between my legs, and tracing it along my cleft.

"Stop!" I said through a rolling laughter, swatting at her hand. I loved it.

"Besides," Maggie continued on. "We used the hell out of this thing and it would have been pretty weird to leave it for that chick to use again on herself."

"It's pretty weird that we used it at all!"

"I guess," Maggie intoned. "You love it, though," she said, snickering, looking at me as though she could read me completely.

"It drives me pretty wild," I said. "It's exciting."

"I know."

Letting the toy flop to the bed, Maggie climbed up and wriggled toward me, falling to my side, slinging one arm over my belly, and pressing her lips thirstily to mine. Kissing her brought me so much joy. I reached my hands up to her face and held on, the two of us lightly moaning as we pressed together. I could feel the desire brewing up inside of me once again, remembering how expertly Maggie had brought me to climax just minutes before. I yearned to make her feel the same way she made me feel.

I slipped my hand between her legs and felt the slippery

satin of her panties, moving my fingers back and forth against her, applying a firm pressure, feeling her mound through the fabric. Just the slightest hint of wetness came through as I caressed her. We were both beginning to breathe heavier through our ardent kissing, chests pressing together, flesh sticking. I could smell a hint of salty perspiration mixed with the recognizable musky aroma of sex.

"I want to fuck you so bad," I sighed out in a breathy murmur between kisses.

"I want you to do that, too," teased Maggie.

"Take these off," I whined, tugging at her panties.

"All right," she said, applying one more kiss to my lips before she rolled onto her back and started quickly shifting out of her underwear. I watched reverently as she did, Maggie pushing the shiny fabric down her thighs, little grunts coming from her mouth, squirming a bit as she got them further down her legs and then rapidly kicking them off as soon as they reached her feet. "How's that?"

"I like it," I said. As though my movements were out of my control, I slipped my hand back between her legs and caressed her front to back, back to front, loving the soft tactility of her pussy, greedy to feel its increasing wetness. I pressed a finger between her slit and adored her.

"Mmm," she cooed, grinding her butt down into the bed. "I think you're getting the hang of this."

"I'm catching on."

As Maggie relaxed back into the bed, I hopped up onto my knees and positioned myself at her side, still lovingly massaging her back and forth. With a smile across her face,

Maggie widened her legs to give me greater access and I took advantage, petting her with more urgency now, pressing my fingers against her to part her lips, exploring her pinkness, watching as her beautiful flesh shimmered with dewiness. I scouted through her folds, admiring, until I brought a single finger up to her clit and slowly began to maneuver it in a circle.

"There we go," said Maggie, eyes closed, grinning. Her arms snaked upward and latched on to the headboard as her hips widened and her legs splayed out further. Lowering my face down now toward her middle, with my finger still attending to her bead, I pressed a firm kiss on her wet lips and inhaled. Maggie's aroma was botanical and inviting. Then I offered her a long, slow lick.

Maggie shivered, body pulsing, a laugh leaving her mouth. I felt one of her hands pet through my hair as I kissed her again, I licked, I suckled. With my palm against her bush my thumb touched on her point, firmly stroking it as I pleasured her lips to lips.

"That's nice, Dana," she whispered. "Oh," Maggie sighed long and low. "That's really nice."

I loved the feeling of Maggie's moistness on my face, my lips buried into her, and I exalted in the taste of her. It was subtly floral, with a light sweetness mixed with something tart or mineral flavored. I wasn't used it to quite yet but I lapped at it hungrily. It made me feel close to Maggie, her flavor, her texture, her fragrance. It made me feel like we had a wonderful shared secret.

Pulling back to take a breath, I adoringly rubbed my lips

over Maggie's fur, kissing her mound, nestling my nose into it. As I did this, Maggie pushed her fingers through my hair, giving me a light tug, grinding her butt into the bed. I could tell she was totally turned on, ready for more, eager for arousal. Little moans came from her mouth with each breath almost as though she were whimpering. It was sweet and it made me feel loved.

I sat up on my knees now, swiftly pushing a tress of my hair behind my ear, and searched around the bed. Maggie had opened her eyes and watched intently. The grin on her face grew as I lifted up the purple toy and showed it to her.

"Yes please," she said, quickly nodding.

Returning my focus to her heat, I let my free hand fall to her mound, resting atop it, as my thumb lightly resumed diddling her clit. Maggie moaned and let her head fall back to the pillow, succumbing once more to the passionate joy welling up in her figure. With the dildo in my opposing hand, I aimed it toward her middle and guided it to her pleated flesh. She was drenched, shimmering, and when I pressed the toy against her, Maggie easily accepted it inside.

"Oh-ho-ho God," said Maggie, her face contorting as she welcomed the pleasure. Her shoulders lifted up off the bed slightly as her body folded upward, quickly dropping back to the sheets, squinting her eyes, mouth open in an 'o' shape. I slowly pulled the rod out of her, watching her flesh grip to it, transfixed by her sex, and then I pressed it back into her.

I started to quicken my pace, my wrist flicking, inspiring a wet melody to sound off from Maggie's middle. It was dulcet, sweet, a thrilling chorus that made me eager to keep up. And Maggie loved it. Her moans entered my ears and made the hair on my arms stand on end. As I penetrated her with that purple totem, a milkiness began to accumulate at the base of the toy near my hand. My heart raced.

"Slow down," said Maggie between breaths. I was getting ahead of myself, enjoying it so much that my pace sped up too much. I looked to Maggie and nodded and she just smiled back at me, her face flushed, sweat on her brow line. I could read the needy lust in her face. "Thank you."

Wrapping her arms around herself now, Maggie closed her eyes and concentrated, her lower half bouncing slowly, evenly, as I continued my thrusting with the toy. Her mouth hung open slightly, her face steady and staid. I made sure to focus some attention on her clit, manipulating it with my thumb, and I could see that whenever I hit her in just the right spot her hips would jerk slightly, her belly clench, her face exude more satisfaction. I could sense she was getting close.

Maggie started pumping her legs, almost getting antsy, and even though I could see in her face that she was enjoying it, she seemed to want more. I wasn't quite sure how to give it to her, I wasn't sure what she wanted, but as I kneeled there on the bed in some sexual trance, my inhibitions dropped and I knew then I was game for anything.

"What can I do?" I mewed. Maggie's eyes opened and looked at me. We shared a glance for a moment before she quickly scooted up, causing the toy to slip out of her though I kept my grip on it. Maggie flipped herself over, collapsing

195

her top half down into the pillows while sticking her backside up in the air. Her butt was nice and plump, thick, pale, slightly reddened from her previous grinding into the bed.

I took a deep breath and ran my palm over one of her cheeks. I was entranced. I exhaled and my breath wavered, almost spluttering, my heart thumping hard against my chest. Dropping the dildo down to the bed, I plunged my hand between Maggie's thighs and fondled her, pulling at her elasticity, running my fingers through her wetness. My arousal was through the roof and I could feel the humidity between my own legs as I praised her. And before I knew it, I was lowering my face down closer to her backside.

"Oh fuck," Maggie moaned into the pillows as I ran my tongue over her rear. She squirmed, she arched her back, she subtly bounced back and forth. At first I felt fear. But as my tongue continued to run over her rim, my hand still between her legs, massaging, tugging, I grew more confident and more steady. I felt like, as I kept on lapping at her, the arousal inside of me was growing leaps as bounds as well. It was a new experience for me and it was immensely exciting.

Pulling back, panting, I looked down at her ass and smiled to myself. I pressed my thumb against her rim, applying firm pressure, pushing down, petting her adoringly. With my other hand, I gingerly slid two fingers into her accepting aperture, pulling them out, pushing them back in. Maggie was juddering and jerking. It made me feel incredible to watch her heave in pleasure.

"So good," she intoned. "So good."

As our lovemaking continued, I grew more courageous

still, beginning to prod at her rear with my finger, running my finger around the exposed ripples. I felt like something novel was happening to me, the creation of some sort of desire inside of me. The more I looked, the harder I found it to look away. My finger offered solid, methodical strokes and it was making Maggie insane. Her body was rocking back and forth, each exhale was a moan. Soon, almost as though I knew what I was doing, I brought my wet fingers up and back, using them now to massage her backside.

I was just in some sexual autopilot. Truly. It was hot and exciting and it was different. I felt like I was watching myself do it, or like I was watching a sexy movie and I was doing what I wanted to watch next.

I switched hands, my left hand moving to Maggie's pussy and stroking it while my right hand, with fingers wet, caressed her rear over and over, firmer and firmer. I was quavering myself, almost shaking, eyes wide, feeling a tingling in my thighs.

"Yeah," said Maggie steadily, her hips gyrating as though she were riding my hands. "Mmm, I'm so close, so close."

I felt Maggie's backside dilate just slightly and before I knew it, my fingertip had entered inside. Just as I started to pet around, however, I felt Maggie's rim clench down tight, her entire middle tightening up, as she began to uncontrollably squirm.

"Fuck!" she cried, shivering and vibrating, hips bucking until her entire body fell down to the softness of the bed in a reflexive tremor. Maggie held onto herself, legs kicking, face gritting, head trying to burrow into the pillows. Her orgasmic pleasure sent shockwaves through me. The connection between us was palpable.

I watched intently as Maggie writhed, placing my hand on the back of her thigh, adoringly stroking her. She would clench, then relax, then do it all over again, sometimes sporadically shifting in one direction. I loved watching her come. It made me feel impossibly accomplished.

Exhaling a deep breath, Maggie turned over and lay on her back, one hand on her own belly, smiling sweatily up at me. I looked down to her and cherished her. Reaching out, I traced my finger along her arm.

"Did you lick my butt?" Maggie said teasingly, wildly grinning, obviously over the moon.

"I did lick your butt," I admitted, feeling embarrassed but also totally flustered. In a good way.

"What'd you think?"

I took a deep breath and thought about it, my finger haphazardly drawing circles on Maggie's skin.

"I liked it," I said shortly, looking off. Maggie laughed contentedly.

"I *loved* it," she said. "Oh my God, that gets me off so hard."

"I really felt, like, when I was doing it," I said. "I felt like *I* was getting close to getting off, too."

"*Really?*" beamed Maggie.

"Oh man," I said. "It kind of felt like this forbidden thing. I don't know!" I shrugged and smiled happily.

"Mmm," hummed Maggie, squirming a little into the

sheets as she relaxed. The room was quiet for a moment, the blankets askew, our naked bodies resting atop it, the light low. It felt like a perfect scene. "Sometimes you just need to open up and try wild stuff to know what you truly like," she said finally.

"I'm beginning to see that," I said.

"Like how you've opened up and now you're fucking ladies! Well, *this* lady," said Maggie, snickering. Then she gasped like she'd been taken by surprise. "Can you believe it? You try the thing you've wanted all along and — *surprise* — you enjoy it."

"Okay," I said, rolling my eyes at her. "I get it."

"I'm just funning around with you," she said, grinning sweetly up at me. "Come lay with me."

Without another word, I slipped down next to her and cradled into her. I wrapped an arm around her and we snuggled, happily coalescing into one another's warmth. A joyful sigh exited my lips.

"I'd do it again," I said after a few moments of silence. "The licking."

"You know how to please a gal," said Maggie, petting her fingers through my hair.

"I just want to make you happy," I said.

"I am so happy, Dana," she said. "Like, really and truly happy."

"Me too," I said. "Really and truly."

We cuddled there together in the soft orange light of the hotel room, our breathing quickly becoming syncopated, hearts joining in the orchestration. I loved Maggie, I loved her as an old friend, I loved our history together and what that meant to my own personal story, and I loved the story we were writing together. This felt real. This felt like it could work, you know, for the long haul. And that filled me with so much hope for everything to come. All the negativity I'd felt in my past, I felt like this thing that was happening between Maggie and I was washing it all away.

"I love you," murmured Maggie, kissing my head, stroking me, limbs intertwined, her words lending to the possibility that she could read my mind.

"I love you, too," I said. I meant it. This was my life and I'd never been more ready to live it.

———

THE RADIO PLAYED at a low volume. It was a melodic tune, kind of electronic but with a slow tempo rock beat. It was comfortable and serene. Outside of the car, however, traffic was terrible. We had only recently made it back to Illinois and it felt like as soon as we entered the state, construction had started. But that was just hyperbole. We'd already made it through a lot of the farmland and were probably just a few hours outside of the city.

Maggie had her eyes focused on the road, one hand at the bottom of the wheel, though we weren't really moving. She bobbed her head along with the music as I sat in the passenger seat, barefoot, in shorts, one leg pulled up with my arms wrapped around my knee. I know we were both tired — exhausted, really, from the trip and all that driving.

The drive home from a road trip is never as fun as the drive out. The drive out, you're filled with possibility. You know your responsibilities have been suspended for a while. You know that you're destined for a good time. The drive home, though, it makes you wish it weren't all coming to an end.

"Who is this?" I asked.

"Yumi Zouma," said Maggie. "They're from New Zealand. Really good, right?"

"Yeah," I said, letting a smile creep onto my face. "We listened to this before."

"We did," she said. "A few times on this trip. I feel like it's become the soundtrack to my life lately."

"I'll have to get this from you."

"I'll gift the album to you on Bandcamp when we get back," said Maggie, looking over at me and smiling.

"Nice."

"This construction traffic is the pits," remarked Maggie, craning her neck down and trying to look further out of the windshield, as though this move would allow her to see past the horizon and find the break in traffic. "Can you see up there?"

"Not really," I said.

"Hmm," she mused.

"What are you going to do tonight?" I asked after a moment of quiet. "I mean, once we get home."

"Laundry, probably," she said. "Wine. I might start putting together this lesson plan but, honestly… I don't wanna." Maggie grinned.

"I don't want to do *anything*," I whined, tossing my head back against the headrest.

"What are you planning to do?"

"Well," I sighed. "Probably laundry, too. But I'm just dreading checking my work email. I bet I'll have a thousand messages to go through."

"You're exaggerating."

"I'm not," I said. "We were gone for almost 3 weeks. You should see how people email at my job. Back and forth a hundred times, saying nothing. God! Let's stop talking about it." Maggie snickered at me.

"Okay, babe," she said. "Vacation ain't over yet."

"Thank you." I smiled at her.

"We're probably not going to make it home for the funeral, are we?" Maggie asked, her voice becoming solemn. "I bet we missed it."

"We did," I said, feeling slightly pained. "My mother texted and said it was fine. You know, they're always generally fine. As fine as a funeral can be."

"Right," said Maggie. "I'm sorry, Dana."

"It's okay."

"It's sad," she said. "But it'll pass, just like everything does."

"I know," I said. "But weirdly, I'm not super sad about it. I guess I'm sad because I'm supposed to be, if that makes any sense."

"It does."

"It's not like I was all that close with her in my adult life," I went on. "So I just... move on."

"You know, it's kind of a blessing," said Maggie. "You don't have her hanging over you anymore, cramping your style." I let out a short laugh.

"Cramping my style, huh?" I looked over at Maggie with rolled eyes.

"You know what I mean," she said with that familiar wildness painted on her face.

"I know what you mean," I replied.

"I mean only good stuff," said Maggie. "The best stuff."

Reaching over, I squeezed her arm lightly and held on for a moment. I felt the connection.

"Did you really tell that girl that I stole her dildo and put it in your bags?" I asked tepidly.

"I really did," said Maggie. "And she thought it was ridiculous."

"So I can never go back there," I said. "I'm not going to be welcomed in Salt Lake City anymore."

"Or..." she said. "Maybe she'll be eager for you to bring it back."

"Stop!" I said through a giggle, lightly smacking her arm.

"Never," said Maggie grinning. "I'm never going to stop."

"It's just what came out," I admitted. "I don't want you to stop."

"We have good conversations," said Maggie after a beat. "I love talking with you. It's so easy."

"I know," I said. "I didn't get mad or frustrated with you one time on this trip."

"Nope," said Maggie in agreement.

"That's reassuring," I said.

"Mm hmm," hummed Maggie, giving me another joyous look before reverting her eyes to road.

I tried to think about what life would be like for me once we got back to Chicago, once I returned to my normal daily existence. I lived on the westside of Chicago and Maggie was on the northside, so there'd be a lot of commuting in store for us. Though I could probably take the Red Line from work all the way up to Andersonville to see her. That wouldn't be so bad. And I could stay over her place, hop on the train in the morning, ride down to work. I laughed internally at myself. I was already planning out my commute from Maggie's place. I felt silly about it but it also gave me a nice sense of comfort. I was excited to be in a good relationship after spending so long being unenthused.

There was so much to look forward to. So much love. So much exploration. I felt newly reborn, in a way. I felt like I still had so much more to learn. And if I was confused at all, or struggled, I knew that Maggie would be there to help me through it. She was such an understanding woman, so much heart, and a keen sense of a humor that could show you the absurdity surrounding you. To help you laugh when you needed it most. Between the death of my grandmother and my own coming out, I was sure that I could use the comforting levity that Maggie was so good at providing.

Soon enough, we'd entered the city of Chicago, navigating the traffic, the construction, the bisecting freeways, until we took the exit for my neighborhood and Maggie drove me toward my destination. I felt a bit sad as we approached my place. I didn't want to leave her. I didn't want the trip to be over. It had been too special for it to end now. If there was any justice in this world, our road trip would have gone on for all eternity.

"No, no, no," I mourned as I saw my graystone house coming into sight.

"What?" said Maggie, looking over at me with some concern.

"Nothing," I said. "I'm just not ready."

"This isn't over," said Maggie matter-of-factly. "Maybe for today, but *this*," she said, pointing between the two of us. "This is just starting, babe."

"I know," I said. "I'm just being bratty."

Once Maggie pulled up to the curb in front of my house, it took a little coaxing for her to kick me out of the car. She, too, stepped out and opened up the back door of the SUV so that I could get my bags. I felt queasy in my stomach. I wasn't ready. I didn't want it to end.

With my duffel over my shoulder, satchel over the other side, and a third bag in my hand, Maggie shut the door with a thud, turned, and smiled wide at me.

"Don't give me that face," she said. Stepping forward, Maggie hugged me tightly. I tried to return her hug but I was somewhat encumbered from all my luggage.

"Kiss me," I said. Maggie laughed and then pushed her lips to mine and the two of us stood there, lips locked for a wonderful final moment of road trip bliss. Once the kiss finally ended, I could still taste Maggie on my lips and I yearned for even more.

"Don't pout," Maggie said. "Maybe you could just come over tonight."

"I don't know," I whined, looking to my bags, looking at my house. "I should get my life sorted out before work on Monday." I then closed my eyes tightly and whined some more. "Stop thinking about work."

"You have Sunday to get your shit together," said Maggie.

"You vastly underestimate how long it takes me to get my shit together." This gave Maggie a tickle.

"Okay," she said. "Get out of here, then." Leaning in again, she planted a soft, sweet, short kiss on my lips and turned. "We'll get together in a couple of days and figure out what the fuck is going on. Deal?"

"Deal," I said lethargically.

"Love you, doll," said Maggie. She blew me a kiss and then climbed back into the car. After slamming the door shut, she leaned out of the window. "I'll watch to make sure you get in safely."

"Love you, too," I said, slinking up toward the house. I climbed the stairs of my stoop, took out my house keys, and slowly unlocked the door. I looked back to the street and Maggie started blowing me kiss after kiss after kiss. I smiled bravely, plucked her kisses from the air and shoved them into my pocket. She laughed, she waved, and then she began driving away. I felt my heart sink.

I CLIMBED the tiled staircase of the somewhat familiar apartment building, the soles of my leather shoes clacking on the steps and echoing throughout the stairwell. Readjusting my side bag, I looked up as I climbed, hand on the railing, taking a deep breath, feeling the speed of my heartbeats increase as I ascended. Outside the sun had set but I felt the light. There was a wine bottle shoved into my bag, among other things, and it bounced against my hip with each slow step upward.

At the top of the stairs I was met with a landing. I turned to one side and inspected the number on the doors. I saw the number 5 and I smiled, eagerly stepping up toward it. I brought my hand up and gently knocked on the door, tapping out a little melody, and then I stepped back a few feet from the door.

I heard the clanking of the wooden door unlocking, two bolts, and then it swung wide open. Behind that door was Maggie, grinning back at me. She stood in the door way wearing her glasses, hair messily tied back, a tank top on with no bra underneath, and worn in striped cotton sleeping shorts. Crossing her arms, she smirked at me.

"I knew you couldn't stay away," she said.

"I was a little hasty in that assertion, yes," I said. "But whatever. I'm here now." I smiled.

"Thai food is on its way," said Maggie. "Pad Woon Sen with shrimp?"

"Exactly," I said. "Oh, and I brought something for you, too."

"I love presents," said Maggie, raising a brow as she watched. Reaching into my bag, I first grabbed at the bottle of wine. But then I reached further in and took hold of something else.

"Here you go," I said, quickly pulling out the purple dildo and tossing it inside of Maggie's apartment. It smacked into the ground with a thud and bounced once haphazardly. As I did this, she squealed and pulled one of her feet from the ground to avoid getting hit. Then, realizing what was happening, she began to crack up.

"You found it," she beamed.

"*Yeah*," I said. "You hid it in my duffel bag."

"I thought you wanted a keepsake from our trip," said Maggie sweetly, teasingly.

"That was you," I countered. "You wanted that thing as a keepsake." She laughed again. Maggie found the whole thing hilarious and, I admit, I did also.

"Fine!" she said. "Twist my arm. I'll keep it!"

"Are you going to invite me in?" I asked in mock exasperation. I went to step forward and Maggie immediately blocked the entrance with her small figure, arm against the door frame.

"Not if you're going to throw dildos at me," she said. "If you're going to throw dildos *in* me, well, that's a different story."

"You're a dildo," I said, pushing past her, pretending to be upset, but loving every second of our back and forth.

Once inside, Maggie closed the door behind us and I could hear her giggling. She was loving it too.

This was everything I had always wanted. This was a real relationship, a real love. Not everybody is lucky enough to find their partner, the person that completes them, the person that makes you be more than you ever thought you could be. Well, not everybody finds that partner on the first, second, maybe even the third go around. But they're out there. And maybe it's someone who's been hiding in plain sight for a very long time. There's nothing wrong in taking your time to find that person, and there's nothing wrong in making a mistake. I'd made plenty of mistakes. I'd been making mistake after mistake for the entirety of my love life. I wasn't going to screw things up anymore. With Maggie, I knew I was finally on the right track.

As we sat together on Maggie's couch, sipping wine, cuddling, plucking at each other in teasing gestures, waiting for Thai food to arrive, I knew that this was for real. This was what I had always wanted. I'd just been too clouded to see straight. Or, rather, I'd *only* been seeing straight. It was only when I decided to give myself a little bit of freedom that I was able to discover who I truly was. And freedom was the best discovery I could have ever found. Freedom… and Maggie, of course.

Thank You!
A Note From Nicolette Dane

I JUST WANT to thank you so much for your readership. I write these novels for you, and I sincerely do hope you enjoy them. If you did enjoy this story, I would really appreciate it if you left a review of the book. Reviews are very important to the success of a book, and your review could help me reach more readers. Even if you're not the wordy type, leaving a review saying "I really enjoyed this book!" is still incredibly helpful.

I have so much more for you to read. Keep going through this book to see some of my personal recommendations. If you enjoyed this story, I am positive you'll love my other stories as well.

Again, thank you from the bottom of my heart.

LOVE,
    Nico

If you want to be notified
of all new releases from Nico,
sign up for her mailing list today
and get 3 FREE BOOKS!

Point your web browser
to the following address
and sign up right now!

www.nicolettedane.com

Keep reading to see more books from
Nicolette Dane!

SNOWED UNDER

Alone in her cabin, during an increasingly snowy winter, novelist Emma Doughty has a lot to work through. As she struggles to complete the latest book in her on-going series, Emma must also contend with remnant feelings of heartbreak and abandonment. And now, after turning forty and spending another Christmas by herself, she's feeling completely lost in life and in love.

Emma's neighborhood is mostly summer homes, and winter is a quiet season around the lake. So when Marian Taggart moves in across the street, Emma finds herself immediately interested in her pretty new neighbor. Marian, recently divorced, is feeling lost, too. But she has a much different story than Emma, and she's eager to escape her past, figure out what's next, and finally live her life true to herself.

Both Emma and Marian feel buried by an avalanche of life's difficulties. As their relationship heats up, can this new romance survive the winter blues, an intolerant family, and an old flame?

Follow The Link To See More
www.nicolettedane.com

ALL GOOD STUFF

Missy Marsh is a minimalist. But with her hoarder mother's recent passing, Missy has inherited a home full of stuff. It's a daunting task to manage, a burden that provokes old memories and reminds her of current struggles. Although Missy has downsized her own life, she now has much more baggage to deal with—both physical and emotional.

When Missy enlists the help of a local estate sale company, she meets Daphne Martens. Daphne is a beautiful woman, and Missy can't help but feel attracted to her confidence and poise. With the guidance of Daphne and her impetuous sister, Missy not only sees a way forward with her mother's house, but with her own emotional hoarding as well.

As Missy opens up and addresses her feelings, things with Daphne take a turn for the romantic. With new love on the line, can Missy find a happy medium between her lifestyle of less and having the things she's always wanted?

Follow The Link To See More
www.nicolettedane.com

FARM TO TABLE

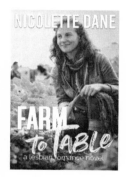

Kimmy Brooks is a young chef at an upscale restaurant in a small vacation town. Although she's made strides in getting her life on track, a lack of direction and low self-esteem has got Kimmy in a rut. She's made it far on her own, but where does she go from here?

When Kimmy meets local farmer Ava Kloser, she discovers an accomplished, savvy, and hard-working woman who seems to have it all figured out. Ava is the kind of woman who goes after what she wants and knows how to make things happen. But while Ava's initiative is inspiring and attractive, Kimmy can't help but struggle with feelings of self-doubt and unworthiness.

Ava can see Kimmy's talent, strength, and potential. As the seeds of their relationship grow and an opportunity for something more sprouts up, will Kimmy believe in herself enough to take the leap she so desperately needs?

Follow The Link To See More
www.nicolettedane.com

BACK ON HER FEET

Lucy Burgess feels like she's lost it all. After losing her job in New York City, she's forced to move back to her hometown with her mother. Living at home in her mid-thirties isn't how Lucy envisioned life. And she's finding it hard to see the light.

But there's hope when she meets Aria Caspar, the pretty local barista, and Lucy's first friend after so many years away from home. While Lucy yearns to return to the big city, Aria shows her all the things she's given up to chase her cosmopolitan dreams.

Amid their blooming romance, Lucy discovers that Aria

has her own challenges to contend with. Can Lucy and Aria push through the loss and heartache together and get back on their feet?

Follow The Link To See More
www.nicolettedane.com

TRAIL BLAZER

As her birthday approaches, Gretchen Slate is looking to do something big. Gretchen is an avid hiker, a lover of the outdoors, and sets her sights on Maine's 100 Mile Wilderness, an arduous and remote hike far away from civilization. And she can think of no better company than her best friend Naomi Benson.

This hike is known to change people, and Naomi is in need of a change. She's never left home, never applied herself, and never admitted her true feelings for Gretchen. In fact, Naomi has spent her life running away from her feelings. While Gretchen is eager to get into the woods and climb mountains, Naomi has her own inner mountains to climb.

Out in the wild, it's easy to open up and be your real self. Can these two friends bring the love they feel in the wilderness with them when they return home?

Follow The Link To See More
www.nicolettedane.com

DIRTY JOB

Mallory Hunt has made a name for herself as "Lory Lick," a professional cam girl who posts videos of herself online in every position she can think up. She films herself solo and in the comforts of her apartment in Chicago, earning a great living and trying to achieve her dream of leaving the city for good. Her job is dirty, but it's also fun and lucrative.

Searching for another girl to join her to appease her fans, Mallory meets Jessi Chappell. Jessi is intrigued by Mallory's openness, and despite her own insecurities she decides to take Mallory up on her offer. But working with someone who makes dirty videos for a living can be a confusing ride when intimacy is so disconnected from a roll in the sheets.

As Jessi grows closer to Mallory, she discovers that this sensual provocateur is much more than she lets on. Could what these girls have together be the real deal, or is it all just for the camera?

Follow The Link To See More

www.nicolettedane.com

POCKET QUEENS

Constance Duke is a professional Texas Hold'em player. She's sharp and stoic, with a steely poker face and a drive to win. The regulars at her local poker room fear her, and the casuals underestimate her at their own peril. Constance is happy making a good living playing poker on her terms. And then she meets Mina Frye.

Mina is a gifted pickpocket, cunning and conniving, and equally charming and beautiful. At first, Mina sees Constance as just another mark. But she quickly realizes that Constance has much greater potential, and as the two begin to fall for one another, Mina convinces her that Las Vegas and the Poker World Championship are calling Constance's name.

As Constance competes with the world's best poker players, moving her way up in the tournament, she must also navigate the secrets of Mina's checkered past in Las Vegas. The magic they both feel is undeniably real, but is everything with Mina just a bluff to trick Constance into going all-in?

Follow The Link To See More

www.nicolettedane.com

Thank you for reading!

If you enjoyed this novel,
please leave a review!

Reviews are *super* important!
Your review can help Nico
reach more readers!

Even if you're not the wordy type,
leaving a review saying
"I really enjoyed this book!"
is still incredibly helpful.

Pretty please?

Manufactured by Amazon.ca
Acheson, AB

11385961R00141